I0797114

Praise for VHS

"Campanioni writes with the zeal of John the Evangelist, fueled by a conviction for the Word as the fleshy wet nurse of our modern reality and consciousness in exile. The peripatetic narrator of this dazzling novel, an American offspring of geopolitical exiles, has taken the trauma of his parents' geographic dislocation and subsumed it into his linguistic and spiritual DNA, into the pith of his narrative bones. *VHS* takes the now-staid modes of much autofiction, turns them inside out, shocks them with a thousand volts of the Proustian instability of the self, and transmutes them into something memorable, incantatory, and wholly original and alive. A bravura performance with a voyeuristic glee that is as much turned inward as it strives to transfigure moments lost in time with the Word."

—Ernesto Mestre-Reed, author of *Sacrificio*

"How can one retrace erased steps to forgotten places? Early in his genre-and-time-bending book *VHS*, Chris Campanioni writes 'There are things not meant to be seen, not meant to be sorted or sorted out,' and then proceeds with searing curiosity to do just that. The framing of the past and the limits of language and stories to capture the churn of life haunt these pages. The blur of fantasy and fact—history—is parsed and pieced together again through intimate reflections on memory, heritage, and migration in this brilliant lyrical and philosophical adventure. A novel as a screen capture, a guidebook, a reimagination, a reenactment. It's an act of love to want to understand one's past, and like all love a mystery. *VHS* gives me everything I want. All those lightning connections of a brain running hot. The mix of tenderness and depth. Jesus. I am so excited for this book to be out in the world."

—Nate Lippens, author of *My Dead Book* and *Ripcord*

"Chris Campanioni has created yet another sexy and stunning book. *VHS* defies categorization. It revels in its rebellion. It is both nostalgic and visionary, an expertly crafted balance between the surreal and achingly familiar dimensions of memory. As raw and unapologetic as Reinaldo Arenas, Campanioni is a singular talent; a director, cinematographer, poet and superb storyteller rolled into one. *VHS* is pop. It's retro. And it has all the makings of a cult classic."

—John Manuel Arias, author of *Where There Was Fire*

"Campanioni's confident, everything-everywhere-all-at-once consciousness refuses to fully take shape or offer clear explanations. Their aesthetics is to ride on desire, memory, and geography, always staying ahead of themselves. This kind of experiment feels antithetical to the more structured discursive forms I'm used to, yet the montage and polyvocality of *VHS*'s narrative both dazzles and inspires me to try something similar. Perhaps a good way to approach a draft would be to spill out memories and future plans, let associations run to their most eerie edges, and then puzzle together the strongest moments into something that echoes Campanioni's form and tone."

—Hantian Zhang, *The Adroit Journal*

VHS

Cover and typeset by Matthew Revert
ISBN: 9781960988386
CLASH Books
Troy, NY
clashbooks.com

VHS
Chris Campanioni

For Desi,

So was it when my life began …

To have a conversation—not the way it is spoken,
but the way it is heard.

LESLIE SCALAPINO, *THE RETURN OF PAINTING*

When I was younger than I am now—old enough to ask questions about my parents' pasts but too young to understand the common exile narrative of self-silencing[1]—I went looking for photographs

---

[1] Instead of telling me about their lives, the experience of passing, or the conditions from which they were forced to flee, mom and dad preferred to tell me about other persons, strangers to me, other lives I would never know except for the spare moments of speech from which these faces were resuscitated and redrawn, sometime later, by the listener. I listened, always with my back toward the hallway, facing the window, so that as I listened, I could also watch.

The moonlight, the virgin lilies, the nun dove, the marquis swan, the princess who was being painted by a great painter next to a flower in an ivory glass. I wanted to know about the angle of the sun as the light leaked in to temporarily obscure half the face of the princess in the painting, and who had hung it where, and what the room smelled like. They went on and on.

They preferred to tell me sketches and anecdotes and quotations they'd picked up while in passage, while becoming naturalized, while placing a mask under the faces they were born with and which they had learned to both love and hate, to stand out and to hide.

The Japanese, I later learned, call it *kodoku*; the lonely gap in between the real me and the masked me.

of my parents before they came to this country and before they were my parents. My search produced another irremediable absence. Instead of images, I had to conjure their stories as if they were memories and their memories as if they were my own.

A little later, not too long ago, I thought I'd begin writing down their stories; once I copied them out, I began to record my voice reading them back; once I heard the stories, I began to photograph them; once I captured each impression and adjusted their exposure, I thought I might as well try making them move again.[2] On the internet, you can find a used Panasonic Omnivision 4-head VCR player (no remote) for fifty-four dollars, plus another thirty-eight to have the item shipped to you. What I like most about these objects is that they receive stories, but they also produce

---

Everything was doubled, I thought, but also displaced, an excess that invited multiplicity, simultaneity. Reading as a form of watching; watching as a way of reading. I remember my father learned English on the radio. And my mother, too poor to afford even that simple luxury, learned English just by looking, a silence that was a kind of mimicry.

[2] All of my father's favorite memories, it turns out, are of movies. Miracles on the screen; whenever he speaks of movies, he calls them "the pictures." A trailer—didn't you know?—is a place for dwelling but also a vehicle for transportation. In Santiago, when he was a child, there was only one cinema, which played only one movie, sometimes for months at a time. Nevertheless, he would sit in the darkness—he favored the back the very back of the theater—and watch what he had already seen the week before, trying to time his gestures and murmurs so as to repeat the first experience with as much fidelity as he could. His hypothesis, a strategy that served me well later in life, was that your body, too, could trick your mind into believing almost anything.

them. The narratives pile up but they also cover up.[3] At a certain point, I forget what happened first; it becomes impossible to find a single source, a first storyteller.

Sometimes I like to believe that there's nothing better in this life than to wait for it. And so I waited to hear, and feel, the suction of the black tape as it penetrated the otherwise silent machine. I slid the cassette into the videocassette recorder. And this is what I found.

[3] A common convergence whenever we consider language as encryption (coded, conveyed). See: Old Church Slavic kryjq, kryti *to cover, hide, shroud*, and its correspondence with Lithuanian kráuju, kráuti *to pile up*.

tracking

eastern promises

I write because I cannot draw the eyelash above your lip, the eyelash floating toward your feet, our feet, as we stand and wait for it, as if we wanted to wait for it to fall, as if we wanted to wait for it to stop falling.

♦

(The rain continued all day.)

♦

How to tell time from the body. I mean the difference between time and the body, the body and time.

♦

I write because I cannot make music. The fingers are right here, in front of the eyes, to gaze at and to touch and be touched. Right in front of the eyes. Whereas the throat is a mystery.

♦

(It demands imagination.)

♦

A singer, for instance, has an unprotected relationship with their audience. No barrier between their voice entering my body.

♦

What I wouldn't do for that kind of immediacy. What I wouldn't do for that kind of involuntary trespass.

♦

How to explain diminuendo in a text. The exertion of getting softer. Peristaltic pre-dawn and my face pressed into the carpet. My face pressed into the wooden beams below. The exertion of getting softer. The book as a flight from the public.

♦

How else how else would I disappear.

♦

I am kneeling here, like you, sweating. Silent. Like you. To stretch back as far as one can go. And to go farther. Farther or further. An indistinguishable point in the distance. I like places I've never been in person. I like persons I've never been. They say this exercise opens the heart.

♦

Like you, I am still waiting for the mouth to drop. Back to something like an original place. As if all things didn't come from all other things; as if everything isn't already elsewhere.

♦

On the crowded F train leaning toward home, I find your voice beside me: I enjoy reading you in migration, dimming between dark and day, rising above ground and down. I mean south. It is always something I am thinking that puts an end to something I am feeling. But sometimes it also happens the other way.

♦

Spaces invent practices. Lest we forget, practices can also invent spaces. I am talking to myself again, but on the train, at least, during the commute, in the middle of day or somewhere in the middle … so many possibilities for reaching out, or for being touched, or for nothing else but listening.

♦

There are things not meant to be seen, not meant to be sorted or sorted out.

♦

I wanted to write about a white telephone booth with glass panels. The disconnected black telephone inside. The devastation of a people. The rituals of mourning. A language I never learned. Phatic act of enunciating grief. The rotary wheel. The wind at such a height. To carry words or let words be carried away. A giving up—but also: a giving.

♦

The point was never the transmission of meaning. The point is only ever to get it down. Or: to let it rise up.

solaris (1972)

On my first Sunday in the city of fountains and waste, I befriended another child, who took me to a place of refuge where several other children and their families stayed, eating and sleeping among sculptures and murals and so many moons. I wanted to hold each egg in my hand, even the ones that skyed above me and lit up the dusty floors and made the constant traffic, when I closed my eyes, sound like galaxies moving about the universe. *(And stars of the sky fell to earth, as a fig tree casts its unripe figs when shaken by the wind.)* Together, we lived in that abandoned salami factory in the eastern outskirts, on Via Prenestina, a name I am still learning to hold in my mouth as I recite what's been written on the chalkboard before me.

pájaros de verano

you stroked my hand, maybe you grazed it. with your own, which was enclosed within mine. (unable to tell then the difference.) with your cheek and the rim of your lips. with your polaroid eyes. with your insistence on asking questions. and it was raining. to be looked at, oh to be looked at in the eyes for as long as this screen permits, the life of a degraded battery. (the terrible certainty of arrival.) I want to remember to say I miss more than just the mirror's patina, ripping the songs of childhood, the waistline of a machine inching toward another enumeration, what of flesh is divisible. when the habits of birds coincided with the view outside your bedroom window, as seen from a hug. (I embraced you from behind.) it's absurd, it really is absurd, how interchangeable a body turns out to be. you asked me why I liked this photograph of you and I pointed to the cinema marquee you were standing under. (I hadn't even squeezed the trigger.) and what a cool clarity in every intentional blur. asking all the time who it is inside of you, who in you has faded out into a telenovela, a curious surface, a text that writes itself, mouth of a single river or this train ride through portable coordinates (the yellow stretch of asphalt that wants to invite precaution), decrepit high rises I remember living in when I was not myself. pájaros de verano. years ago, my father, who printed out our conversations from the internet. when I first left, when I was in london, when I was at the checkout or returning home with groceries, answering questions in russian (by nodding). to resuscitate the past and make it material, in expired deskjet ink. the betrayal of time or just time zones. permit these arousals, these certain indiscretions. lo-fi fantasies at roller-rinks, hands on a joystick, melting into each other on a balcony overlooking the lesser-known piazza del duomo, et cetera. the volcanic breeze of june. to become or to have been is out of the question. I can't help but recite quotes from memory. from what I can forget, which is the same thing. what happens is the mind goes first and then and then the beautiful breath. if it's raining, if the rain stops, will you know it by the way the faucet drips and drips or does it. if it's raining or we put our heads down, if we held our hands out, would we feel the same, not exactly ever the same. (a tear erased, a water that tastes like flour. give me just enough to lick the image.) when I wrote this I was still living, annotating on the F (a damp bench, the view of the city at dusk), and later, sitting at a desk that doubles as a dining table, or the reverse. to eat isn't it is to work with words. to feel each shape as it curves against the teeth. when we zoom in, when we move on (each other), when we come this close, all a face becomes is a buffering horizon

field of dreams

The wind carries voices and the bodies they belong to across the divisions of red or the impossibilities of orange. The self-assurance of cherry opening in broad daylight.

A city passes hands.

I am a researcher of uncertain discipline. (My double identity.) I am also a child, longing to see home, perhaps for the first time.

I heard that when someone or something disappears in our world, they do not leave an empty space but rather a chain of connections—a stump whose spectral limbs branch out in several directions. So my first miracle was the miracle of sight, of staring at people and seeing how they acted when they did not know another person—if it's true I am a person—was watching.

So the woman wants to know if I have a preference for my top and my bottom. She says, with a gesture of which I am unfamiliar: pistachio first, or French vanilla? So I was beginning to think of my words as colors and my sentences as gradients.

I had that old habit of getting younger all the time. When I arrived in this port city whose river opens into the sea, I was still wearing the clothes I had been given in wardrobe, the gray cardigan and tweed trouser getup whose function, among other things, was to facilitate my passage as an expert in a particular field of study. Which field? The numberless tracts of rye on Bernauer Straße at the corner of Ackerstraße, which at one time served as a liminal stretch of "no man's land" comprising inner walls, protection barriers, minefields, observation towers, alarmed fences, barbed wires, and dog patrols, is among my current favorites.

Whether or not I had actually aged, what was true, at least, is that since turning twenty or twenty-one, I had begun to mature toward childhood. What pains me is my freshly printed identification card, which causes an alarm to sound every time I sweep its magnetized edges against the lobby's turnstiles. What pains me is the lack of Oxford comma in the 1987 comedy film *Planes, Trains and Automobiles.*

My department chair, here at the university to which I've just arrived, says everything I say is a little bent. What do you mean? I ask, except we aren't speaking, preferring, instead, in the weeks and months before I'd arrived, to talk over text. Like me, A entered this country as a visitor, on a provisional work visa, except that he decided to stay, camouflaged, as I've so often been camouflaged, by the gloss of expertise I nevertheless despise. Between us, our stew of Englishes—borrowed, imitated, imaginatively jammed and slapped (together)—remains susceptible to per-mutation in other tongues. So that is why I'm here, I imagine, or at least that is why they brought me. Just as the river swells and drains, so too does my notebook. The university, or its board of trustees who paid for my appointment, were interested in what leaks out. So A, too, looked younger in person, except we had never exchanged photographs, and I'd never bothered to look him up. So we were each attracted to *jetztzeit* for the sonic qualities it offered in our rudimentary German: vigor, undisciplined spillage, current and undercurrent. Except the *jet* is really a *yet,* as in addition, repetition, continuation, or emphasis: the intensification of presence which may or may not be [still] occurring—e.g., *I have not finished writing these notebooks, [yet] this may happen in the future.* Time at a standstill, in which the discharge of past, present, and future evacuates to the event of speech. Now-time. There was once a Walter Benjamin who'd inscribed *jetztzeit* in his "Theses on the Philosophy of History," a text that incited his denationalization from Nazi Germany, a text that remained unpublished and itself in transit, when Hannah Arendt brought it in her baggage when she, too, passed through Portbou, months after Benjamin did, suiciding on morphine pills after ordering five lemonades to room 4 on the second floor of Hotel Francia.

I sat here, in this field of dreams which is actually a Eurocash Cash & Carry parking lot, and contemplated what other memories would be stored in my camera eye tonight, and would my reader like them. To grade papers or to read or to write poems or to do nothing but sit here in the incandescence of Eurocash's window display and the periodic wind and my one-beer body, to allow the four-point-five percent alcohol to permeate my flesh and whatever's underneath, to let it leak and dribble. The blackbird wants to be yellow. My organs want to be a different shade of pink.

I awoke, at some uncertain hour, mouthing Cold War coded radio transmissions with my left foot asleep and my right hand still clutching the rented camera phone whose image gallery I'd spent the morning dredging. If I timed each occurrence and graphed it across this page, a flowchart of our internal rhythms might begin to impose itself over the narrative proper.

Now I rely on the violence of white, the voice-over intoned, a surface in which everything blends.

On most Boeing 787s, Business Class passengers receive an extra shoulder strap attached to the seatbelt encircling their waist. What this means, in the event of air carrier failure, and the possibility of crash, is that the bodies of Business Class passengers will have a greater likelihood of being decapitated prior to impact than their distant Economy kin, owing to the velocity of the hurling aircraft and the sudden decompression of the plane's cabin, which, taken together, would turn the nylon shoulder strap into a shank. Aboard a failing piece of floating titanium, hardly anyone in Business Class ever dies on collision. So many of the deceased, I heard, remain safely secured in their seats.

What was the weather like that day? We can assume it is autumn with the thickness of her long coat and the blouse that she is wearing under it.

When asked which of this nation's fabled scribes I'd most like to see broadcast as a walking, talking hologram, I mispronounced "Goethe." When asked about my methodology, I told A, my department chair, it comes fast or not at all. Fragments of sensations, conversations, and anecdotes cut up and broken across the lines, details that did little to make the sketches more legible. I wondered if my notebook was actually a cosmologist's journal. I wondered if these notes were coordinates. Susceptible to weathers outside me, time mapped to the act of speaking, your voice laid over the image track. What's on your mind, I think I remember replying, and what comes to mind.

It may have been morning with the amount of light in this photo.

Hours later, while trespassing the city archive after closing hours, A will tell me that the DDR stood for Der dumme Rest, and when I will have heard this, I will have laughed. Although I know very little German. And the joke, if it really is a joke, will be lost on me. In another novel, A would start consulting a personal trainer, because I really want, he would often say, at least one vein in my forehead.

In the photo above the mantelpiece, a man with dirty blond hair (thick and tousled) crosses his right leg over his left, reclined on a deckchair overlooking his modest garden: chrysanthemum and marigold and the turquoise of his high-rise jean shorts, with the incomprehensible stretch of gray a few feet behind him. In the man's hands is a magazine or a pamphlet or possibly a notebook. Possibly he is writing in the notebook as he stretches out in the middle of the day with his feet in slippers and his socks on, picturing the other Berlin behind the walls, imagining a stage set that does not include a ninety-six-mile concrete border at his back.

The aptly titled Todesstreifen (death zone) can still be seen in many places. Some of them are large areas of brown, uncultivated land. Some are now parks. Some are now parking lots.

On the trail of my parents' exiles, I remain susceptible to detour. As a boy, he used to marvel at the sounds coming over the telephone wires when his mother handed him the receiver, and he murmured the handful of words he'd learned in Polish, to speak back to his mother's uncles and aunts and cousins, who called him, once a year, and always on the same day, to sing a song that translates, roughly, as a declaration to live one hundred years, and one hundred years more. He thought, if I have that amount of time, surely, I'll one day meet all the family I've spoken to but never seen. Surely, I will one day return to the two places where I come from and which I have never been.

There is a blank space here, something he doesn't know, or has misplaced, perhaps intentionally.

Some years ago, well before I was appointed to my temporary post, hired to lecture on or in my uncertain discipline, a ministry for renaming appeared: Polish was substituted for German; streets were given different names; names were stamped in a different typeface, with different diacritics. In my memory (my imagination), this occurred overnight, instead of—as is the truth about almost anything imperceptible—in broad daylight. All the old signs have now been restored or replaced. All the old Germans who were once Poles are Polish, I guess, again. So every origin is a myth. So every separation could be a link.

So I often, as I walk these streets and conjure their erstwhile alphabets, etched, like a palimpsest, somewhere underneath or below the present, ask myself, in my slightly bent English: At what point before death does a body forget itself as a body, at what point does the body absolve the mind of fright and terror? And when the person has been reduced to a body, and the body deemed incompetent as either commodity or consumer, consumer or labor, what is the breaking point, or is there any, for the body's exploitation after death?

While I was napping, a federal judge in Chicago rejected arguments from attorneys for Boeing that the airline carrier should not have to pay for the pain and suffering of one hundred and fifty-seven victims of a March 2019 Boeing 737 MAX crash because the passengers of Ethiopian Flight 302 had all died on impact.

By the time you read this, Saturn's iconic rings will have disappeared. I'll be on a flight to Athens, where octopus is prized among all the creatures of the sea. Wondering all the while about the metrics of life passing into death, or what happens when the body disappears from the record of the law, the law of record. How do we begin to remember what is missing?

In the gardens between the districts of Kolonaki and Pangrati, where, in evening, the Acropolis is spot-lit by the moon and eco-efficient LED fixtures, I run, bedazzled by the scent of citrus blossom and the musk and funk of my groin, the night breeze drying my damp flesh if I pause long enough to record this, rescue it from an uncertain oblivion. I prefer the night air, the way the city sounds at twilight, how the body, too, seems to disappear alongside the mind that had already been borne by exertion, repetition, the aforementioned scent carried by the creamy white flowers mercilessly planted amidst the arid air of the Mediterranean, where so few of the five hundred species originally imported by a German agronomist have survived.

Haven't you ever heard how an octopus must be handled before it is to be eaten by eager hands? First, the creature must be shot in the head and then, once stunned, brought to shore to be beaten to death against the jagged rocks. Because discerning diners expect only the most succulent meat, the fishermen will sometimes take an alternative method to death by stoning, placing each octopus, one at a time, in the washing machine until the body has been tenderized and the creature has been rinsed of all life.

In Athens, and on the island of Naxos, where Zeus, in this very cave, was said to be raised, I marveled at all the bodies frozen mid-stride, nude and ruined and unashamed. I like to think that the figures etched in limestone and marble are not broken or incomplete but uncompleted. I, too, am without shame.

roman holiday

We rented *Roman Holiday* and took it out to better see our faces. Stickers still adorned the plastic. I felt the shell and thought about protection, and a little later, what it meant to steal. A price I still can't name or why we chose this one from every other, glistening in the halogen-lit aisles. We wanted the world and the world in black and white. Classic and romantic, the way all dead things are.

We placed it on the dresser and began undressing. One opening at a time, deliberate and metrical. It was as if you were taking notes or I was only watching. The flesh beating. The shadows on the wall. We hadn't even thought to press play.

It's sad to furnish you with what you already know. Audrey Hepburn, Gregory Peck, a ride around the Forum against a golden backdrop. Something celebrated and familiar. Faces to freeze like that.

I regret not having a voice to give you. Some soundtrack with which to move along, the same one or similar to what's playing as I write to you, or you write to me, and I speak the words you've written. I would have liked to provide another means of transport. A way in or a way out.

Our Roman Holiday resumed on Eastern Parkway, three stops on the red line and two blocks walking. Probably I imagined we'd been riding a Vespa instead; her arms around my waist as I steered and smiled. Sometimes all it takes is music and the insides of your eyelids. Dark, of course, and all the light in the world.

Outside, still dark. Still and dark. That purple-pink dark before the black settles in, swaths the clouds and stars and everything. All the light in the world but also stillness. Deep and penetrating and capable of being cupped. Nothing but nothing. Everyone at work or at home or at the movies, maybe watching the film we'd rented. All of Brooklyn still and silent, the way a moving image sits before a trumpet blares and the credits roll.

One by one by one by one.

We enter or appear, careful not to get caught as the glass pane pulls in, pushes out, lets a stranger pass. Even the carousel scared me as a child. Something about returning. The same but also different. Carousels still scare me. Sliding doors. Escalators. The pause between floors in a moving carriage. Going up or down?

We walk in and walk out into another room, another room that leads to other rooms and the smell of nail polish, panorama of sculptures and artifacts, objects and drawings. An obsidian mirror that asks us to stop looking.

A work of art should arouse a physical sensation. That taut feeling in my groin can rise, at times, all the way up through my throat. What I want above all is a convulsive beauty; I mean the kind of beauty that flutters in and out of frame in the moment before a finger lingers. Aims. Depresses. Something capable of making all the air go. Choked and stuttering and somehow even quiet I want to die in that beauty. I want to live in that beauty too.

None of this is on display the day we arrive, on Vespa or by foot, scouring the dead as if we'd really been raiding tombs all this time. Isn't everything an excuse for rupture? You called me depraved once and I began to believe it; I saw the evidence in my own eyes looking back at me when I took the disc out to examine the silver edge, the part where all the footage goes, everything worth watching or everything that's been filmed to watch later, in another room or another life. We move from room to room and the view opens up in front of our eyes, shifting as the light shifts, gliding like water or flooding the floor with footsteps, careful to step on each crack, the thin line between tiles where guests often leave receipts, a proof of payment or passage. Everything worth looking at should be looked at close-up; I mean in the face. I wait for the epiphany like I'm reading a mass-market novel. And when it comes it's because I've stopped reading. Here we are at the cathedral. Here we are at the forest's edge. It's really as if I am lost and these things have come to give me some news about myself. Say hello and tell me more. First, how about a question.

We took a Roman Holiday and didn't remember why we wanted to be there in the first place. What a thrill it is to leave ourselves, briefly and without explanation.

The point is not to pack anything at all.

until the end of the world

Before I am allowed entry and because I am allowed entry, I am asked to show my face.

Well, I'm gonna be happy to get back to reality. (Four days later, in the same airport, at a different terminal, a man will turn to me and press on.) *And when I get there, I'm gonna have to figure out how to pay for the fantasy.*

my fair lady (1993)

everywhere and everywhere
I haven't been, I've had
to tell myself in passing
make moments, not money
I am tempted to say this
definitely did not happen during the
intermission of *My Fair Lady* in 1993. I am tempted to say there was a period of my life where I stopped counting footsteps and started to subtract them from the parabola of my encounters

elsewhere I've kept dedicated records of even the things I should have done

glances on the street and faces I still follow from afar
have you or have you not
tried printing out hard copies of the internet

I am tempted to say
what I want to say
every time someone asks
if this much, why not more?

I am tempted to say this writing takes the form of a cosmetic pill that you consume, fragrance excreting through the skin's surface, redefining the particular vibe you've likely outlasted in the years since birth, remember

make moments, not money, and then begin counting
the ways the way
water counts stones

this wall features proposals, suggestions, and ideas
for restricting waste and refuse and for inventing
new forms of production and consumption

write yours in the notebook provided

writes yours in the space between words

write yours as you wait for my text and wait

to hit send
must be willing
to die for me on my online
dating about me

I am just another american
falling asleep
to the television I am tempted
to say

what ever happened to clipart, the careful quiet before a wish, to
walk into a party without knowing anyone and not know anyone

come to think of it to think of it
I come without having to
do anything but make you
in my own image

what does your face say when your face says nothing?

return to the moment after the moment
has been erased

return to loneliness what
an uncommon gift

dangerous liaisons

E falls in love with M, whose real name is A, A who is pretending to be J, J whose images glut the internet the way certain US Americans hover over the omelet station at a hotel buffet. When the ruse is up (it's gone on for far too long; they haven't even FaceTimed), E finds J through J's sprawling images (like looking for crumbs that form a sacred path in a forest), alerting them to the game of (missed / taken) identity. E and J talk, artlessly and unabashedly, without restraint, without ever having to speak, across salty bodies and oppositional borders and unshared languages and conflicting time zones. Meanwhile, A, still playing at being J (under the assumption of "M"), professes their love, bares their (real) face, wonders how they could have ever lost the love of their life to the person they'd been all this time pretending to be. Translation, A claims, or blames. A problem of translation. J gets on the next flight (in E's mind, it is always *the next flight*), meets E (in person), who falls in love with J, who falls in love with E. Sometimes it happens without knowing when or in what order. In variations of the story, J is renting this liaison by the minute. I prefer the French, the way a silent consonant at the end of one word can suddenly sound like it begins the next word when that word begins with a vowel. I want to insist on adding the word *dangerous*, which is how E will describe A, after learning that A has been using photographs of J to become M, all the time asking, without ever having to ask: *is to fall in love a form of decapitation?* Some questions never leave us, even when the people behind them do. A turns their attention to another subject-object, another scenario they can produce or to which they might participate, leak out of, like any life. The possibility of something real inside every fiction. M is the only one still inside the text. I imagine I to be their reader.

planes, trains and automobiles

Trying to write for class, my student writes, is like convincing your dentist you've been flossing. When did I stop flossing? When did I stop growing up? In this scenario, I am the dentist. But maybe I am also the patient on the table. And maybe the table is the text. And maybe language is the floss moving in and out of the gum lines, as each syllable jostles or maybe gyrates up against the flesh, when it's really good, when you're doing it right.

On NPR, a doc today about twins, displaced from their native Germany during the Kindertransport of the late 1930s. Arriving in London they receive new names but also a new past. Too young to remember who they are or from where they'd been evacuated, they grow up with no knowledge of their mother's murder in the death camps, or the fact that their father was an officer in the regime that sent her there on the numberless trains paid for by their own doomed passengers.

Like in the room of this photograph, I am sitting, my right leg folded over my left, between a wall of books and the terrace, with its potted plants leaning toward the open window, the autumn sun.

I like to fill myself, to open the hatch and absorb, the way I open the hatch to extract words, and when I'm not filling myself, I am emptying myself out, so often having to piss and shit that I require an endless supply of locations on my virtual map, should I be running errands without pause from morning to mid-afternoon, labeled as "watering holes." Perhaps I am not a monster so much as a man, since ninety-two percent of men regularly spend at least twenty minutes on the toilet, a fact I gleaned from L, who sent me the infographed stat while I was sitting aboard my American Standard Cadet FloWise, looking at an ad titled looking for a Gay Man to take my wife out to party (Chelsea).

My wife is great, but she always wants to go out. Especially to Brooklyn electronic music events. Unfortunately, I'm unable to keep up with her and would like someone who can chaperone her to these events as a friend so I can get some rest. Ideally, you're into this type of music, you like to party, and you are probably in your late late twenties to thirties.

I include this here because, like my father, who pretended he was anything except Cuban when he arrived in the US amidst looming nuclear war launching from San Cristóbal, where palm trees were thought to camouflage Soviet missiles, I want to appeal to a wide audience. Which is another word for the verb to survive.

How, I ask my students (I ask myself), can we produce a narrative through negative space? Of what is not or no longer here, of what did not or has not yet happened, of what we may never return to, never write about, account for, but for these lines that desire betrayal and betray desires for a brief encounter, dazzling zigzag of consciousness when consciousness pauses to recall the preparatory arrangements of near occasion, unripe incident, like a memory of an experience that does not exist but could exist, might have existed, does.

This photo was taken by a photographer named Peter Leibing on the fifteenth of August 1961, near Bernauer Straße. The captured moment shows H, a young East German border guard tasked with guarding the construction of the Berlin Wall, who, taking advantage of a moment of distraction by his colleagues, escapes to the West by leaping over the barbed wire barriers that mark the border between the two Berlins. After the photo was taken, that is to say after H leapt across the gnarled divisions of his homeland, he became a refugee and began a new life in the Federal Republic of Deutschland. What happened to the border guard turned refugee, in the years following his daring escape and integration into the West, as members of the Stasi continued to exert pressure on his family and loved ones in the GDR, except that he crossed back over, legally, after the fall of the Wall in 1989, and not ten years later, had hanged himself at his home, where he lived alone, but for a few scattered photo albums, and the library of books he had begun to collect at the numerous second-hand shops that sprang up throughout Berlin, as if overnight, following Germany's Reunification.

When and in what capacity, I write across the magnetic whiteboard, can we find a use in apparently useless things? And underneath this, in the same blotchy black sprawl provided by the cheap dry-eraser markers huddled together on my temporary desk, half of them dried out and drained of ink: When objects have gone out of use, what happens to their identities as subjects?

On the air today a commemoration of M, who was cloud before the Cloud, patron saint of lost media, an early Apple investor who used her money to record every minute of TV news from 1979 until the day of her death in 2012. Ten years later, we can watch the seventy-one thousand VHS and Betamax cassettes that were originally stored across her nine properties and three storage units on the world wide web of our imaginations, had we but world enough and time. Like certain persons obsessed with railways and timetables and directories, and the logistics of interval and duration, M's family outings were always plotted around the length of a single VHS tape; every six hours, when the tapes ran out, M along with her husband, and later, a trained assistant, would switch them out, across no less than eight separate VCRs installed with the expressed objective to not miss a single moment of air time, including commercials and credit sequences. Sometimes I feel as if I've become another M, convinced that there is a lot of detail on the air or in the air at risk of disappearing forever. And I would have to—haven't I?—arrange my life in accordance with the tempo of each message's vestigial broadcast.

Whenever I am in movement, synchronized with velocity and delay, I bring several stacks of messages with me, re-reading old birthday cards from station to station with the same degree of fascination held for the *Arcades Project* or the collected lectures of Lacan and Merleau-Ponty.

In another book, I'd wondered about the alchemical quality of writing as a mode of transcription and transformation. In these (as in all) scenarios, I don't have a life so much as I have reproduced it. And it's the copying out that matters. In this way, I've become nothing but myself, and I needed to imitate myself to better become who I am. Sometimes, I write, I had written, I have the thought that when I write about what happened, I might change the outcome—that is, change the future but also the present and the past. But just as often as I believe in the benediction produced through the conversion of passing thoughts into printed words, I also ask myself (I ask you): Does writing an experience down devalue it? To the extent that it reduces skin and sensation to the syntactical arrangement of parts of speech written, even in the darting stream of notation, always after the act; that we (I am including you, here) live through the most ecstatic and horrible moments of our lives just so we could write about them later.

And just as soon as I asked this question, I heard, or began to listen for, the low slow drone of the AC that often aided me in sleep, as if I were being massaged with the same dust cloth with which I rub the blur against my eyeglasses, to rub it in, to take blur with me. The crispy skin of an apple, the running water, the cool flesh, the sweet aftertaste, the bruised peak, the metallic liquid with a solitude I take for granted, a body I've never questioned until recently, an aging face, aging eyes, eyes that aren't mine, seeking so often repetition as a mode of difference, the low slow drone of me coming back to myself. Grief is not the correct word for the condition into which I have fallen, through which I have endured all this life. But if not grief, then what? It would seem (at least to him) that he had the gift of always being remembered, or of forming memories in place of experiences.

I slipped into other dreams that evening, other versions of the same or similar, the main plot interrupted by scenes and episodes I nevertheless recognized as a spectator, as if I had only ever been watching, vignettes and scenarios that threatened to overtake the feature film of my subconscious. In one, I was no longer wandering the Paris Arcades or the Jardin du Luxembourg, where the same lovers sit on the same park bench, day after day, year after year, at twilight, waiting (or so I like to think) for me to walk by, and my own waiting, for them to slip out of their hand-held ritual and say hello—always expecting others to acknowledge my own desire to be alighted upon—nor was I running along the stretch of South Brooklyn's tree-lined Ocean Parkway, but wading against the current as the sky began to open above me, a moment during the year, however brief, when the seawater here turns pink along the eastern edges of the island.

I am only eighteen years old and have moved from place to place, where each time I must learn to adapt to different behaviors and expectations. I still envision relaxing, as a five year old, with the people I called my cousins on their yellow terraces while the rain poured. I still envision the two red umbrellas that protected us from the enormous droplets of rainwater and how, nevertheless, we still got wet as the water dripped from the rusting aluminum roofs to which we each had given a name. The sounds were pleasant to me, and I was beginning to learn the distance between the rhythmic rain's collapse and the crashing thunder brought by dazzling flashes of light. The musky smells that the night storms offered were pleasant, and however I'd be feeling throughout the day, when the moon was in the sky, sitting with my knees up on the yellow terraces that we each shared and where, in the evenings, we all met, I felt refreshed.

As if these photographs and postcards and letters and the notebooks scribbled with fragments of narrative, verse, to-do lists, aphorisms, overheard conversation, and quotes transcribed in passage were a magnetic field, and what was being dragged toward one another were not objects but the time they each contained: the past shuffled with the future and the present until each voice melted into a kind of murmuration, and it was impossible to tell who speaks; of who is the speaker and of who listens, and in what arrangement is to be laid down the order of events.

Tell me about a day you woke up in another place, on another chronological frequency, in another time zone, I'd instructed my students hours earlier, inside the glass-curtained vertical campus, so named because of its fourteen curving stories above the ground, the frenetic city street. Describe the temporal-spatial discrepancy. Detail, I'd insisted, the interval between shock and (re)adjustment.

As every hotel room became a place of transition, in which I could assume other lives, other parts of my identity I had worked to hide or which I had involuntarily let leak, I had a desire to continue such dreams I had left off for many nights, many years … and if not dreams, then desires, since my mother, too, or so I imagined, never had a story of her own, that the greatest adventure of my mother's life was surely (it seemed to me) to be crossing first the Baltic Sea, and then the Atlantic Ocean, as a child on her way to this country that I can and cannot any longer recognize.

Likewise, every day he seemed to become less and less of himself, unless he was returning to who he was from a vantage point that no longer existed, shifting the lens again and again and again and again from which we see ourselves … nevertheless, always at a distance from a home that had now become, like all images that stand in for their people or places, wholly imaginary. Recalling (again) the remove produced through re-writing what has already been written in the third person; of watching old family videos and the failure of memory but for the scraps of evidence to testify to the body's presence in an event that seemed, all the same, never to have happened, unless that was the body's testimony: the certain uncertainty of the body's disappearance. I had by then found work as a teacher in the city where I was born. Between classes, I'd sometimes try to count the number of blocks that separated the college from which I organized my seminars and the hospital bed where I was born, and where I stayed, for many more months than is to be expected of a newborn baby. As I collect and organize these notes, and all the voices that they contain, I understood, perhaps for the first time, that underneath anger is sadness, that underneath this set was another one, and underneath that set, another, and so on. As he spoke, he held his face in both hands, so I had to imagine what his eyes looked like, or the trembling of his lips as I listened.

good time

What kind of boss would you be? a friend asks. They don't know it but I am looking at the cover of *Life & Style*, at the checkout of a Walgreens on a main street in a small suburban town in New Jersey, where Keanu Reeves, Mariah Carey, Jennifer Hudson, and Charlize Theron each and at the same time smile back ... Hollywood's Best and Worst Bosses in glossy yellow font cutting a border between faces, including my own. I want to type back, I disavow power. I want to type back, I'd rather be sacrificed. I am here and I am not here. The attendant behind the counter asks if I need anything, she says, besides the card in your hand, which was in her hand a moment ago, which was in mine. The drama of experience. The tingling of description. Or shall we walk a little longer in view of oblivion—before thoughts ossify, before words penetrate the mute surface we've each glided against, as if bulbs of garlic on the cutting board. I want to be the wood and also the knife. I don't want to be sentimental. The intonation of a bicyclist's salute as they whoosh against my stride. (Some of this takes place later.) Unrecognizable, like every glance I give back to myself as I walk under domed surveillance. An itch in the throat, against the thighs. I want to be rock from inside, M writes back. And water without. Excess of the male nipple (the poster of a shirtless Rob Lowe hanging in Corey Haim's bedroom), something I hum incidentally as I walk onto the F, at Jay, just before sunset, the swell of emptiness, cars without bodies, windows without eyes. When I think of you, like that, I want to cherish the face of the stranger whose voice cuts across my ride, in the midst of movement. In the midst of hip and drizzle. What it would be to have the patience of an ice cube. The exchanges, without remorse, that contour and say nothing.

vision quest

On the day I was to pick up my new glasses, I was late for work. Would the new glasses, I thought, as I waited for the perpetually delayed uptown F to arrive, disguise my tardy presence? Would the new glasses turn truancy into a form of celebration?

At work, where I so often stand at the center of a room with my masked face on full display for rows and rows of persons, sitting at their desks, watching me and listening, or playing Candy Crush Saga (prior to its untimely discontinuation) on their phones, I placed the glasses over my eyes for the first time. No longer late, I thought. I am au courant.

You look like the Matrix, a student says, as I unzip my leather jacket and sit down. I want to ask if they mean the philosophical concept of a simulated reality or the film. I want to ask which one. I want not to look like the most recent one, despite its technologically advanced cinematography, its meta jokes that never(?) get old.

♦

My favorite thing about my new tinted eyewear (Day 1) is the heavy-duty double-lock "High Performance Resin Case" (made in Italy) with which to carry them, when I'm not carrying them on my face. Grasping the black brick by its lunchbox-like handle, I might appear as a technician, or maybe more specifically, an electrician, ferrying important and possibly illegal electronics across micro neighborhoods of the Financial District, zigzagging Fulton Street, where everyone is either wearing a backpack or a suit. When you get down to it, when you get down in it, like Trent Reznor in "Head Like a Hole," the alchemical nature of all tinted eyewear is that they make you feel like someone who is always *doing other things*. What those things are remain a mystery, even to the ones doing them. (Just then, a tiny little dot caught my eye. It was just about too small to see, but I watched it way too long; it was pulling me down.) Remember the strange warping and propulsive drumbeat that heralds the song's opening, the prominent synth shifting into what might be mistaken for an adult human's groan? Think of your habit of becoming a spy whenever you travel; the thrill of being under the covers, while in plain view of unbeknownst passersby. In these sunglasses, I can be both Jason Bourne and Trinity, Holly Golightly and the sexy stranger you've just welcomed in, to fix your Verizon Fios router. Vampires—didn't you know?—require an invitation.

I suppose in the end or at the very beginning, that's what this is all about. Wearing your sunglasses at night and during the day serves the freedom to look without permission, without discretion; in that unequal gaze is the survival tactic of verbal-visual code-switching, where space is negotiated through refusing one's audience the ability to distinguish between appearance and disappearance, seeing and being seen.

As you debate that hypothesis, I've been Googling the difference between hackers in real life vs. hackers in movies. (Search results confirm there is none.)

I return to my new glasses, or my new glasses return themselves to me. On the downtown F, I receive a tap on my shoulder; a woman lets me know my backpack is open. My eyes might betray a sense of embarrassment or surprise, but my new glasses hide all, even the optical expressions I'd like to convey. I once read a think piece, the woman adds, pointing to my new glasses, on the significance of eyewear for your sense of self.

What's the difference between a piece and a think piece, a thought said in passing and a passing thought?

I want to continue this conversation, but I have to switch lines.

♦

My glasses have names. Koharu Eclipse, Nagata Speed Blade, Comfort Logic, Calm Tech (a sibling? a rival?). My favorite is Tinman Elite. When I am wearing Tinman Elite I feel more cyborg than human, spectral but also material and maybe even bossy, or boxy, in a sexy unravelable way, composed of dozens of main frame wires, cords, and batteries, an eroticized assemblage of parts, so many of which are unknown to the user who enters the scene of pleasure, androgynous and android-ish, a popular choice for any writer, we who are only ever halfway here.

In District Vision, I emerge in Friedrichshain, at an East German pharmaceutical factory turned dance hall. I've just walked in. I am looking for you. I am looking at you but you can't see me (I'm in disguise).

Strobe lit cheeks and eyes I'd like to eat in evening, if I hadn't already been fed on what District Vision offers me. "Neue Welt" by Dascha Dauenhauer and Max Rieger bounces off the club's walls and everything starts to accelerate. The song's chorus screams, or maybe that's the crowd of darkened bodies huddled upon my gyrating thigh. If you're near a screen or stereo, you should turn the volume up.

How are you enjoying the DDR? I whisper.

What's the DDR? You mouth back.

The brand of my favorite bar of body soap, I reply, leaning closer in the hopes that my District Vision will leak out. I want to suffuse you with DDR era restlessness and my erstwhile profession of canine escort. In other circles they call me "puppy." What other circles? We're in Friedrichshain (or Kreuzberg, or Prenzlauer Berg) shortly after I was born but before the Walls fell. Do these glasses, I wonder, allocate lethal doses of nostalgia? Aren't all doses of nostalgia, I write back, lethal?

♦

I walk into a store that announces it is looking for a pedicurist in its shopfront windows. I, too, am looking for a pedicurist. When I am not wearing my new glasses, I am playing tennis, and so my feet, particularly my big toes and the stretch of sole that connects metatarsal to heel, are maligned with calluses that have rifted my skin in ways I would otherwise be reluctant to describe.

Maybe, I think, if I wear my glasses as I play tennis, I will prevent these unseemly foot sores. I will no longer be looking for a pedicurist. I will instead only be looking for a safe space to rest after a particularly grueling "hit" session, without sitting on my eyeglass frames, and accidentally morphing them.

♦

If I were my glasses instead of the person wearing them, what would my origin story be? What was the name of the person who fitted my blanks into the lensometer; whose hands determined my lenses' thickness and contour? What did the successive stages of fine grinding, polishing, and shaping smell like? Where did I come from? How did I get here?

♦

Sometime in the past, or the future (depending on what day it is you're reading this), I'll meet T, and he'll relate his aspirations to create an intellectual access point for people, a bridge into the world of outdoor wellness that does not begin and end at Dick's. This was in 2016. Weird things started to happen in the meantime. Guys started to walk around, T says, pointing to my feet, in HOKAs. My legs are nodding, the way they always nod when they are under a table. It will never be known how this is to be told, from the perspective of the table, or my sneakers, or the cloud of leaves that gathers at the curb and floats past them.

♦

When I am not wearing Tinman Elite, I am thinking about them; I am thinking about walking around the banya in them; they might as well be here, on my face, as I stroll from steam room to sauna, sauna to ice bath. At the Mermaid Spa in Sea Gate, I did not wear a black T-shirt emblazoned with the phrase:

Best Massage! Andrei Serkolov

That shirt was worn by Andrei himself, who tried, without success, to provide me with the best massage of my life.

♦

What makes me qualified to write about these Takeyoshi-inspired performance eyewear other than my chance encounter with a glasses-clad companion, who'd passed them off to me while skateboarding through Tribeca, days ago or moments after? I became custodian of the heavy-duty double-lock "High Performance Resin Case" (colloquially known, I think, as HPRC 2100) and entertainer of the eyewear they contained after a photo of me on an exercise bike, wearing nothing but blue briefs and a red headband, unexpectedly went "live." I am no more alive than you, who encounter me in the text. It should go without saying. My new glasses are your new glasses.

♦

Behind every glasses is a pair of eyes, and every pair of eyes belongs to a face. Needless to say except it's so often unsaid, since mass production obscures the possibility of transparency, since what is the assembly line but a funeral dirge, burying the presence of cultural exchanges and their contributors. Little Lamb who made thee. Dost thou know who made thee?

It means something, in the language of Japan, to have your name on an object. The object becomes a dedication to the subject, unless it's the other way around. Look again. Maybe the object is no longer an object but a meeting point. District Vision. We had no product when we launched, says T, when we are sitting outside the Marlton Hotel under a tented patio, I without any objects on my face—the glasses he and M designed—so I can look at him in the eyes as I type this from imagination or memory, which is the same thing. It was just a place to do things together. And each name would be a gathering point. New York City would be a district. Mexico City would be a district. Tokyo would be a district. What I wanted, I remember thinking, was to create more online opportunities to push us offline. When does an object, I write down in response, assume the form of a relic, a talisman, a token (an omen)? When does an essay become an itinerary?

♦

When I walked into Blue Hill Farm off Washington Square Park wearing my tinted eyewear, the woman who greeted us at the door, just before the bar, figured I was visually impaired (I am). A short time later, as I continued walking, winding my way to our lavish booth, a word I often use in incorrect scenarios (so often wanting to attribute extravagance to the ordinary), I was thought to be a celebrity (am I?). Rough hypothesis: if I continue to operate my gaze under the assumption of chiasmus, then I can smuggle parallels and intimations into hum-drum relationships and disparate coordinates. To walk into the Michelin Star townhouse in tinted eyewear is to appear as if you mean business. But what does "business" mean in the context of an eight-course "Family Meal"? These glasses hide my hunger; they hide my greed. I wrote *hide* but maybe I meant to write *absorb*. Comfort Logic[4] absorbs my anecdotal repast, returns it as aura.

If we were still watching, this would be the part where narration halts. I don't want to tell you what you already know; my new glasses furnish the public with information that would otherwise be *for your eyes only*. In fact or fiction, I am sitting here, at the collapsible Target-harvested dining table that doubles as my work desk, vibing to my Discover Weekly in my old glasses, prescribed for my convergence insufficiency, my tendency to duplicate single objects, as if everything that exists exists to be reproduced. Doesn't it? When I write, like I am writing now, I get giddy. Words turn me on, but they also turn on me, in the way that language always returns us to something we could be feeling if we give up ideas about control and ownership; in other words, if we give up ideas about the singular and individual. I could be adapting this missive as a screenplay; I could be directing your actions, as you reprise the role of Tinman Elite, and conjure the soundtrack that will later be overlaid on the image track. Isn't that the point? For writing to become film, film to become sound? For words to become everything they are, which is empty. My new glasses, too, await to be filled by other faces, more levelheaded than my own.

[4] A style of frames I named myself, as if I were the subject and its author, tasked with creating the eyewear I am also writing about. Isn't all writing conditioned by the face-first plunge, but moreover, the hole that begs perforation and leakage? What comes first is exactly the point.

only lovers left alive

Why does it have to be a plain white wall, she thinks, knees up near her chin, in a bed both old and unfamiliar, the mattress sagging at the center and the threadbare sheets scratching at her skin, floral wallpaper is a good touch, but I wish there was paintings. Actually, she thinks, as she turns over once again, now her left cheek pressed into the wilting pillow, it would not matter that much, how walls should be—their tendencies and behaviors—is not something I ever think about when I look at my ceiling, or the ceiling that I now have above me.

Her eyes gradually began to reopen in the night, facing the green, paintingless wall, a wall that doesn't look green now because it's dark in the room and color-correction wouldn't come till after. It was too late to read a book or talk to ghosts, but it would be light soon, wouldn't it? The sun would be up, maybe already is, and mama would be on her way home from the factory, having created all that toothpaste, all those tubes, and the beets and potatoes for our meal would be needed, and the gray stockings unsewn, so what is the point of sleep at a time like this. At least a window, she thinks. Give me a window, so I can see the shadows of the cars passing below, or the lamplight flickering at the corner of Diamond. The sun in her blue-hour position in the sky.

And I do not have control over my thoughts, she thinks, now her right cheek pressed into the pillow. My thoughts, she thinks, have never been mine since I came to this country, or probably before. Since I graduated from przedszkole, since I stopped learning about my body, since I locked myself up. Whenever I would see something exciting, she thinks, I would calm myself down by thinking I'll go dancing eventually, I'll learn cooking eventually, I'll get good at drinking coffee eventually, I'll be able to talk to people eventually. So there's no need (she thinks) to think about them now.

I thought to myself: being suspended in space after going through a black hole is something I have imagined a few times. I thought to myself: when I say something I wanted to say in the company of other people, I feel most like a person. People pay money to get the gut of their dreams, she remembers overhearing, head bent low while awaiting her name to be called—a name like and unlike hers, a name that couldn't be pronounced by the men in this country—as bodies began to fill the windowless room, the paintingless room, she thinks now, with something that resembles a smile, extracting the stuff from their best friend or lover and planting it in their own body, nurturing the mysterious garden, plotting the meshes of neurons, which line the gut with microbes and all the bacteria they harbor, synthesizing chemicals that make us happy, or the reverse. Or that's just how she imagined it, at least, in another tongue. For who knows what the body does below the flesh. For who knows what desires a person might have. In another life and another life, I heard we will regret the ways we hardened into awareness, into muscle and bone.

In bed, or what passes as a place in which to temporarily rest, she remembers the announcement of a name, and lifting her head to stand, walking to the woman behind the counter to hand her the white slip of paper she'd been given when she'd arrived. What seemed like hours ago, or days. So long had she been waiting, learning to look at people and their gestures and remembering them for later. The way their voices sounded, the tempo of a sentence and the stress on certain sounds. And then the questions themselves, knowing the responses after so many rehearsals that while her mouth moved, she was free to think about other things. When I speak, I seem to have a mouth. I assume I have a face as well. I feel my lips and my teeth and my tongue and it all feels, she thought then, looking at the man in the suit in his eyes as she continued to narrate their reasons for being here, in this country, in this country and not her own, very natural.

Maybe her stomach rumbled. Maybe she regretted the coffee she'd prepared earlier that morning for the occasion. Maybe she wanted a new gut. Mama's friends had sponsored their stay in the United States, but who among the handful of people she had met here could she turn to for that kind of request? A new life to go with this new country, that was not her own but could be. All the other waiting days, vestibules and lobbies, ugly rooms with neither paintings nor windows, the W is actually a V, she had practiced saying, the W does not exist. How could you expect another person to believe in the presence of things that nevertheless remain unsaid. And the woman behind the counter who did not look up as she received the white slip of paper and muttered, third room on the right. It was the second room, actually. And since she never looked at me when she spoke, I wonder if it was a mistake or some curious insult. And since we arrived here, on the very top of the place that prepares bodies for their second death (their second birth), how many people have I met while trying to sleep, while trying to think, who are no longer alive. Here and not here, depending on one's view of things. And how different life would be if I was a back sleeper instead of a belly sleeper. All that air up there with my arms dangling at each side, the freedom to face the ceiling, if I wanted to, she thinks now, knees up near her chin, if I felt like looking back.

news from home

There was a kind of feeling, there, there was a rush and a hesitation. There was the earth moaning as I revolved my hips and tilted my neck back, or the reverse. There were ice pops and the swollen taste of wood and the smell of chlorine; maps of cities and road trips. Now I transport my body places. I move from A to B (and also nothing). Now I count the days and collect videocassettes. And this glass of water nearly empty. And the way the water shakes in the glass as I write and because I write. I've been told I am, I guess, a very physical writer. Maybe what you meant to say is that I have an aggressive penmanship. I like to really feel, I guess, the imprint of the face as it is slapped against the arid, thin skin. Since everyone knows that a perfect mediation is the message that disappears in the act of being sent. So we asked ourselves about whether or not it was so strange, after all, to desire newer and ever more dazzling machines, and our equally propulsive wish to escape them. Or maybe, with a kind of feeling, to forget, after we'd already become fully integrated within their fibrous cables and wires, that we haven't also escaped ourselves. The unnatural sound of a head hitting the floor, the head having already left the body. And the train conductor's voice, humming on the audio track. It was like tasting from another's mouth. He asked me about my appetites and I told you, as I ran my damp hand through my dry, wind-beaten blond hair, I'm attracted to junk, which isn't the same as waste, which isn't the same as the eternity hidden inside any object that asks to be named.

We rode on the elevated train and I parted my lips wide very wide because I was so full of confidence. Just a day before, I'd found an ad-free instructional video titled "how to smile like a human being" and I was already putting it into practice, moistening my throat with the back of my tongue and applying my jaw, too, without straining my lachrymal sac, another trick I learned, years before, from a different video.

The last time I went diving with you, your friend had a beautiful wetsuit and you asked her where she bought it. I read the anonymous note back as the recorded thunder roared again and the rain began to slide down the window glass, so close to your cheeks as you leaned your head here that it looked as if you were crying. Though when I stopped to think, to write this down, I caught my own face looking back, blank look in the blue eyes. Insert an ad-libbed description of my torso, wreathed in a ragged white tank-top threaded with holes where my belly button might be, where my navel might have been. Another passenger—someone I've never seen until today—chimed in about my tendency to give off California vibes. If you watch her cheeks move, if you pause, here, and hold the frame, you'll notice that the line has been dubbed. *I was born of things*

[beat]

that are not a country. What I am saying is that you can tell a lot about someone by the way their lips uncouple and compress, and with what cadence, what tempo and intensity when they speak; when they say things they'd never intended to say or had wanted to say, or never actually said. The letters continue like that, offering updates about everyday life at irregular intervals, despite the likelihood that the sound of the letters being read would eventually be drowned out by the engines on a four-lane boulevard, somewhere on the Upper East. So the Japanese are on my screen, rediscovering their faces as they stretch the sides of their mouths upward with their fingers. So I coax your fantasy of acid-washed jeans spinning on the checkered floor like a fresh CD-ROM from my rolodex of thoughts and sensations, remembering, as I do, not the Gospel of John and the nativity of the word but that, in the end, all we had anymore were images. By the time you get this, we will have left the set, descending the stairs toward the flooded streets, thinking how every nation is a crime. We will have vanished alongside our machines in perfect, frictionless movement. We will have stayed up all night, rewatching *News from Home*. What comes after?

memorias del subdesarrollo

Lineage of a wave in motion. The palm swaying softly like an ass. Lineage of the desire I felt before me. I mean prior to being. Borne.

♦

How to travel (like) light. How to say good-bye to the skin you thought would save you.

♦

I made a note to look up *apophenia. Bootstrap paradox. Parataxis.*

♦

I am starting the only way I know how.

♦

I made a note to say good-bye to the oil-stained sheets. To say dispersal. I knew I had a taste for it the moment I tasted it.

♦

She says wouldn't it be nice to have memories of the future? She says I would never forget all the things I have yet to do.

♦

I'm always torn whether to mark this movement or to let it ride untouched.

And you feel pleased very pleased to be on the move again.

When I was young or younger than I am now I used to dream about the two places I had come from; the two places I had never been, except in stories. I'd sit and listen really listen to my mother and my father as they described the kites from the roof deck, with a view above the sea, or the way the ducks in the farm looked at dusk, before anyone else was up to see them and I'd see them differently, listening really listening but also shutting my eyes so I could picture it again, from my memory, which is to say the memory of the one who listens.

Fiction as transformation (of the raw material). Nonfiction as proximity (to the event).

I don't often have to remind myself to be always writing somewhere in between.

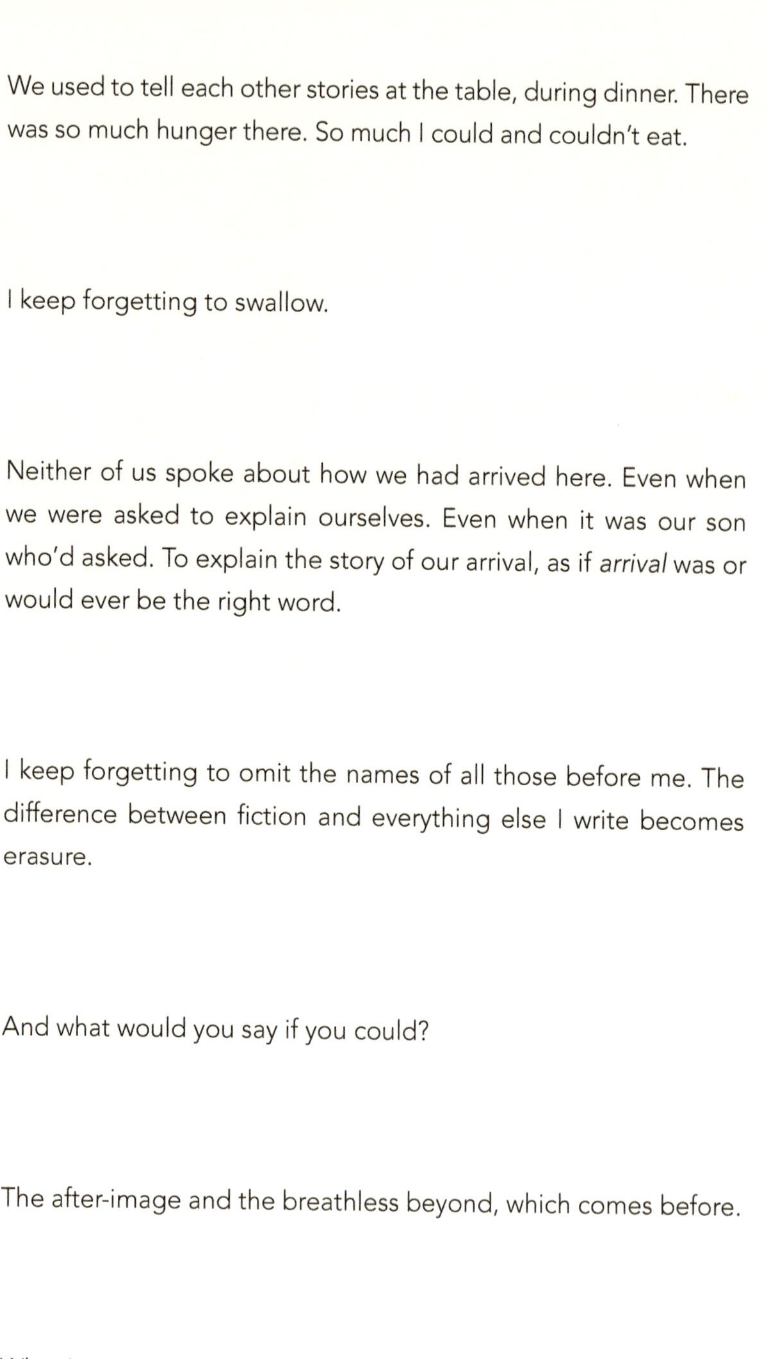

We used to tell each other stories at the table, during dinner. There was so much hunger there. So much I could and couldn't eat.

I keep forgetting to swallow.

Neither of us spoke about how we had arrived here. Even when we were asked to explain ourselves. Even when it was our son who'd asked. To explain the story of our arrival, as if *arrival* was or would ever be the right word.

I keep forgetting to omit the names of all those before me. The difference between fiction and everything else I write becomes erasure.

And what would you say if you could?

The after-image and the breathless beyond, which comes before.

What I am trying to say is in fiction I don't omit anything.

We used to tell each other the stories of our passage, forging what we wanted to forget or turning inward when we had nothing really nothing to say. It's sad, I often think, to have to make it up as you go. To not have a past to return to.

How else how else to honor ellipsis. The curtailed comma.

In dreams I remember being born in the water, somewhere between the East and the East (again), but differently. Confluence of the Caribbean and the Vistula. A body I've had to name to know. I've heard dreams have a tendency to trickle out.

She took days—no—years to write.

I wanted to be the one who remembers.

I often think about the coincidences that make up a life. And every etching reveals something, also, underneath or behind it, something that was always already there.

I write fiction by stitching together my essays and articles. I write nonfiction by plundering my novels. It's a game I like to play, or else that's how I think of it, how I like to think of it: a game of graphing and grafting, a move toward defamiliarizing the real and rematerializing the fantasy.

Sometimes this duration is inevitable, even necessary.

Marking can mean *demarcating*. And what I want is autonomy, not unity. Indefinite profusion. Permission of mutual substitutions.

And if not the memory of the one who listens, then who? And if no one remembers, where else where else did we come from?

He liked the wine from Corsica. It tasted of the sea.

true romance

My story begins with a lack of legibility: some unfamiliar handwriting on an envelope addressed to me, or at least bearing my address. I had only recently moved in. It could have been meant for anyone.

(ever notice how
showerhead video
reviews resemble
amateur porn?)

The teeth, I will later learn, are placed in a hazardous waste container and, once the container is picked up at the dental office, incinerated.

I dream of all the teeth, all the gums and tongues they've fondled or been fondled by; all the gaps and cavities, mouths like shafts, faces like holes.

(the clarity
of a 69)

I require …
intensity and eroticism
tenderness and aggression
vulnerability and subterfuge
excess and inadvertence

(similar conditions include Fregoli delusions, in which one believes that various people are actually the same person in disguise; Cotard's syndrome: the belief that your blood or organs have been absconded with or that you don't exist at all; and reduplicative paramnesia: the sense that a familiar place has been copied and substituted)

on an otherwise
innocuous monday

mistakenly sending my super
a nude

post internet's hypothesis was we could fall
in love with someone whose hair we hadn't ever smelled before

post internet's hypothesis was not that
your very close friend could be a simulation

but that the simulation could be
your very close friend

(the artist is nothing if not an imitator)

people tell me
I give good paw

Early in the twenty-first century, technological advances have made it possible for aging, wealthy people to pay crooks to go back in time, kidnap young adults and deliver them to the elderly clients, who then have their brains transplanted into the healthy bodies.

To be forgotten, to be settled and dead; to be setting the table, my mother, my father, me, my brother, whom I never write about but why I haven't ever asked myself in text. What it would mean, how I must love them all the way. A promise after all of this acting I want only to stumble off stage into someone else's set (so I did it myself and it feels nice), becoming for a life the only thing I ever allowed to hold me.

(Brad Pitt is watching Emilio Estévez on the screen but who is watching Brad Pitt?)

The memories are painful. Sometimes I believe not even death can clear the mind. And then what? I was asked to write a short composition about what happened to me and about my first impressions of the United States of America, this country to which I do and do not belong, where to walk on the street is to be hailed all the time and all the time to be hailed differently. It is very difficult to really answer such a question because my experiences and feelings are so many and widespread that I could not describe them within the frames of a short story.

In the photograph my mother is the only one dressed in white, a hooded cape adorning her face. Before a forest or a shrub or a hallucination of bushes and trees (a river I can only name). When I look again, it is no longer my mother's face. When I look again, I, too, have moved off the page.

total recall

What role does the camera play in the story?

One thing most people don't consider is that the underwear you are or are not wearing right now has been intended for a body that is not your own. For the last fifteen years, I've fitted for a diverse list of fashion brands, putting on and taking off countless samples sent from India and China and Thailand, so that the factory originals could be tested on a breathing body, against which each garment could be cut or lengthened, and each error manufactured by men and women and their children in precarious working conditions could be amended before shipping the product back to the West, to be sold to consumers at an uptick with the soft metallic sound that portends every sale. If you happen to own a pair of men's underwear purchased in the United States at any point in the twenty-tens until today, each measurement—from the inseam and leg openings to the back rise—was designed to fit a single body, which is mine. At these fittings, designers and their buyers and each of their assistants take photos, thread pins through textile, flag marks on the material with chalk or blue masking tape, and sometimes, even, turn to the model to ask questions about how something feels; how it feels to be a body inside this fabric. In these spare moments of interrogation, stacked with the prospect of a product's swift recall, I'd often consider fabricating my experience, relating some spectral discomfort, or describing how ideal the gusset looks in a piece whose pouch is already imprinted with whiskers, hoping, I suppose, to pass along a glitch in the universal model, which was my own.

I had been reading from my notebook, but also adding notes, periodically, and it was soon difficult to find which passage I had been looking for in the first place, on this cool wooden bench, with the yellow lamplight's nimbus above my head, just before it was to begin drizzling, when the rain would speckle the night air like a sequence of commas or semicolons, the haphazard coordination between stage set and studio control room. It was much too loud to sit inside the bar, and anyway, I prefer the aura afforded by Little Fuzhou—how the wide and busy arteries of Canal and Ludlow abruptly melt into this alleyway on Division Street with the lit-up apparition of City Hall behind my shoulder, in the shadow of both bridges and the elevated FDR Drive, my notebook still in my writing hand. Maybe, I thought (without writing it down), my notes weren't meant to be retrieved but rather reconstructed according to the whim of their reader, or the conditions from which they arrived at these discrete and nonconsecutive moments, to turn them into liquid co-incidence. And so soon did I consider the ways in which I depend upon form as a kind of camouflage did I acknowledge, even for a moment, the several and various layers superimposed upon each other, like the skin's seven membranes or a good lasagna, which, taken together, became this city. When the radiator kicks in later and I'll close my eyes, trying to trick the body into feeling the heat surge through each opening like quarters in the pants pocket or popcorn coming to its logical conclusion. The papered faces of victims plastered against the concrete or another disappointing eclipse. It would seem (at least to him) that he had the gift of always being remembered.

They say that when the leaves fall so does your hair. The animal with whom I live is also beginning to shed. I do not want to decide between redemption or reckless and unforeseen debasement. I can convince myself that this is enough, ghost in the glass, the way my shifting companion looks at me, when I think to look back at the window above my hip. To be aware of yourself without fright. But maybe a certain degree of fright, together with other unnameable things, is necessary for this task. Sirens and another floating train rumbling in the distance until the laughter cuts back in. If I pause the frame and mute the volume, I can picture the waterfront of the East River half a dozen blocks away, and the careless gestures of the current as it continues to nourish the renovated esplanade, where people sit with their hands cupped, knees beginning to bend, opening themselves up to each other for the first time.

I feel inside my leather jacket's left pocket and retrieve a receipt, unwrinkled as if straight from the printer. Kale, bunch. Fresh peeled garlic. That's it—that's the whole purchase. What does it say about me, I wonder, what does anything mean until we give it meaning, clothe it with associations and symbolism. I remember to write this down. All the things you could be doing if you weren't where you are, which you're not. As if anything that could be called to mind could be enjoyed. I slide the carbon copy back into my jacket pocket, deciding not to trash the residue, so to speak, of my market value. Sometimes, I think, I feel as though it's the useless things that bear the most meaningful revelations. It reminds me of the aspiration to write a whole novel of inessentials, the minor and unnecessary details of encounters that should be forgotten, like all good things, in the body.

I will tell you how it felt for me.

masculin féminin

There must be a word for this. Algorithmically appealing. Or: the lure that allows people to be themselves, while pretending to be me.

I sweat whenever my body asks me to.

Conditions for flight: a gag or spasm in the thighs, like the sound of a stranger brushing, as heard through the walls.

A long torso. Long arms. A long stretch of back. Everything reads long except for my face, which says nothing.

(If I knew what kind of face I had I wouldn't ask.)

In between or somewhere around this I will paint you a composite picture. We can then say I have arrived. And briefly. Film sliding off the reel and reinserted. The changeover which depends on the space between breaths.

Not with a bang, nor with a whimper. But a deep deep sigh.

(Some sounds are no longer with us.)

The click my eyes make when I put a finger to them. Flesh to flesh. Closest thing to an out of body experience was the distant attention to your text. I mean in the way I would re-read it and substitute all the names. All the markers and places, and the persons they contain or do they.

I like to fantasize about the questions that began this interrogation.

If I were asked to return to the subject of shape, I would say my lips are expansive, the wings of a butterfly or the stroke itself. I have a tendency to wet them, by placing my tongue to each rim, so long as we're talking.

Law and Order. The Strain. Billions. Blue Bloods. Bored to Death. Damages. The Following. Law and Order: Special Victims Unit. Law and Order: Criminal Intent. I can handle a plot the way I handle a bar of soap. And if it does the work, it's meant to vanish into the periphery. I'd run—I ran, I am running; time gets funny when you think to write it down—from a certain stoop on the corner of Hicks and Joralemon down and around the Promenade, film permissions on every corner or every corner I think to look: slips of white paper pasted to a pole, overlapping and imbricated, as if one set were interrupting another, spilling out against a single cloud and the midday breeze and the sound of the Staten Island Ferry hovering, if you could call this *hovering*, further down, nearly outside the frame, the *Spirit of America*—not a taxi cab yellow but something darker, with a hint of rust—as extras switched roles mid-scene; plot holes meant to be filled in at random, on accident.

I imagined that my acting career didn't end, when I'd decided to stay in New York City, in 2010, but that it only had begun; it only, I thought now, was beginning to begun. And I looked for myself, passing through so many programs, so many different narratives, which were the stories of others. And I could watch them, later, one at a time, or several in the same moment, on so many different screens, along with everyone else, so long as I paid my cable bill. Or had adopted the credentials of a friend's streaming account. Which meant that I could watch myself only if I pretended to be anyone else.

the lives of others

I would be sitting across from my lover, I would be sitting across from someone whom I used to love, I would be loving someone else, I would be holding hands with my lover, I would be walking hand in hand over the Lover's Bridge, along the Seine and watching the haze accumulate over the water under the shadow of the Louvre, watching the bicyclists and the roller skaters and the skates themselves, as if the legs had walked off the set or as if the skates had a soul of their own. I would watch the stagehands shift scenery, without applause. I would be sitting here, across from you as you describe your day. I wouldn't say much. I would be told I should take more risks. It is I who am telling myself. And it is the telling above all that matters. Think everybody think, I would always want to add parenthetically. I would be planning a party. Guests would already be arriving by the time I got home. The way food shows up for every season, and now the calendar would say fall. I would come bearing candy corn and an umbrella. We wouldn't have had rain in ten days. Is that an emotional truth? I would think but I wouldn't think to ask. The rituals of burial would be so familiar they would no longer be terrifying. I would still worry about all the old women in my life. My mother, my aunt, my dog. Maybe it's because, after I'd turned twelve, there were no longer any old women left but them. I would question if, in the photograph, you are turning toward me, or if you are turning away. I would want to ask you out, to make you dinner, to share my favorite meal. In this and all scenarios, I would be having my cake and I would be eating it too. I would make a list of all the things to say and questions to ask. I would call at a time I think no one will answer. All of our unbearable silence. I would sit still so I could better pay attention. Falling in love is the only fun part. I would answer any question you asked of me. I would answer for myself, all the things I've done or wanted to do, wanted to be doing. It's been more than two years since I've bled. For instance. What would it mean to be forced to let something out? The joy of delivery has kept me inside all day. When people stopped sharing so much personal info on their social networks, social networks responded by introducing an algorithm into their newsfeeds. The name for this phenomenon would be called context collapse. From the Latin *collabi, to fall together, to slide*. More at *sleep*. Other responses would include the opportunity to Go Live, and color-coding one's thoughts. I would be receiving Top Stories without even having to ask. Vegas killer's girlfriend: He was "a kind, quiet, caring man." Republicans open to banning "bump stocks" used in massacre. Vampire breast lifts are the new beauty fad. I would like to ask you to guess which Top Story interests me most. She expected to get high but only, she says, a little bit high. This in response to my question about what you would be doing if you weren't doing what you are doing right now. Another way of phrasing this would become: What's on your mind? I wouldn't have to check myself, because everyone already is watching. I would cite quantitative methods, scholarly research, comparative analysis, my Most Viewed Video Content. Couples who are childless, I would say, live on average ten years less. I am always afraid I'll die before the next line. I don't want to explain why. If I thought to look back at her face, I would see that she was crying. One thing which excites me, in reading this now, is not knowing who is speaking to whom, of who speaks and who listens. The intimacy of anonymous encounters, even in public, comes from the uncertain awareness of not knowing if I'm still me, or who else I've become.

Of who else is becoming me, and how. Has it ever happened that you would look at an old journal or message thread and not recognize the one writing the notes? I've forgotten to put down all the happy ones.

weird science

Could you clarify this matter of things by starting again and imagining me as the person who inhabits you? If the world is weary, it is because I keep wearing it on my own skin, my own breath and blood.

Better to be incestuous. Better to be innocuous. Desk chairs, ice cream cones, a light bulb, a telephone. The long, slender partition of a printer that keeps the paper from piling up. Overflowing. Think of tía, abuela, mamá—and say it just like that, *mamá*—the clerk at the CVS you frequent around the corner, the department secretary—Nancy?—pretend you're picturing them naked at the moment of climax so as to avoid it, withdraw deeper, surrender without really surrendering anything except time; more of it, infinite thickness of time to be inside of it; put differently: I want to think about applesauce instead of thoughts. Inventing scenarios and small victories in order to endure this little death.

And when I—in an interruption or interference, in the street insurgence of an anecdote, in the flits of lightning that streak through your blinds, at times—ask to empty myself inside you instead of on your bosom, your belly button, on the small of your back, in your mouth, on your cheeks, against your lips—I can really understand what Rilke meant when he wrote that dying and being born can exist at the same time. That we carry our own death inside of us, and at the same time, we carry our own life. And we don't own either.

And to own beauty is the first lie of it.

And so there are times you notice the landmarks you ignored in real life are actual places in movies.

Bethesda Terrace, for instance. We sat in the grass on a blanket and watched ourselves the way dirt watches rain. Click. Click. Click.

take everything—there's no way to
know now what will
be important
in the future

Let the taste of applesauce last ... let it linger even as I write this from the ghost of tomorrow. (To isolate a moment always implies a detachment.) And it seems like I love all of my partners much more after we've parted. And it seems like what I long for is what I no longer have; what it is no longer possible to have. (I am right now longing for the prime rib.) And so it sometimes works in reverse. How I can so easily get myself off just by sliding my thumb across your face. And when we meet in person I can hardly bear it.

Are you bearing it?

And the wine will make this better. And waiting makes everything better. And wishing while waiting might be the whole basis for living. The temporal promises of animal meat. The difference between having and being. The difference between having you in my sight and seeing you as you would otherwise be seen, when I'm not here to look.

"My meat is to do the will of Him that sent me."

(The rib that quotes Simone Weil when it lands on the kitchen counter, waiting for the hands of the one who will bring it its deliverance. The rib that is delivered to me and that delivers me.)

But I want to fasten onto you the way I fasten onto language. I want to experience you with all of my parts. I want to take myself apart in front of you, in plain view.

(We'd met at a bar and exchanged information. I'd been dreaming about this for weeks.)

Things got out of hand, she said, as she placed hers on his rectus femoris and took a deep breath. (She was relating the debauchery of last night's office pizza party.) Je suis l'empire à la fin de la décadence. And the flesh gives and takes it away. *And contact with the sword causes the same defilement whether it be through the handle or the point.*

If death itself is a performance, it is one in which the audience participates. I mean the mass-goers, all of us sitting here (when I try to retrieve it) and sobbing into our hands, or staying silent even as we're thinking about filing our taxes. Or how to prepare the cassoulet.

I was right to fall on my knees. But only because I truly wanted to receive you. And I give you this only so I might beg it from you. (This is the second basis for being.)

Remember how I interpreted your hips involuntarily? To bookmark your photo so I could look at it later, and look at it whenever I wanted

to look. *You strike the match*

and already the noise is you. A parable for any good exit strategy might look like the inside of a private plane, the moment a window breaks. Who struck which match? (In this scenario, I am the fire.)

One time I said my greatest pain in life is not being able to see myself perform live and I really meant it. The exact words were: I don't know for sure but I wish I could see my face. (I end up wishing for this a lot.) In a *New York Magazine* interview, an admirer of mine says he doesn't like to call himself an *environmentalist* because it sounds too radical; he prefers *superhero.* The exact words were: I'm a guy who cares about people. Acting is my day job, but at night, I get to be a superhero. (It's evening, he's talking to a reporter, the two are drinking mezcal sodas at Roberta's. They've requested the absence of straws.)

It's hard to place blame on anyone in this scenario.[5] The mezcal, The Lonely Whale Foundation (a group of environmentalists, according to its website), which huddles around the pair, the effects of Your First Burning Man, the private longing for straws. The fact that this conversation is being taped, played back, transcribed. *I went to this new land.* And that's the thing, my admirer continued, sipping from the rim, shaking his head empathically. It's captivating, because it's unlike anything I've ever experienced. And I'm worldly, he intoned, as if reading from my notes. I've been around the world.

(Remember that most people are not actually looking for anything while they are browsing. They are simply checking to see what people are saying.)

---

[5] And so *I should look upon every sin I have committed as a favor of God.*

And so I'm left with gravity. Inertia, entropy. A desire to pull myself lower. A desire to debase myself in public. A hunger for degradation. And maybe just hunger. The use of temptations. The burden of having equipment and sometimes being equipped. And look: *a prime rib pathetic in its confidence that it was still pink.* Recount everything: a doorman, a revolving door, a streetlight that seemed to pause at yellow, a real life taxicab

confession:

some people are doing it and some people don't
know what they're doing

(An explanation of the New York City art world)

I write you an email. I text you a poem. I cap things off with a self-portrait, beside the shower. In view of the sink. I think about who you are and who you were before you met me. I think about how you've already changed me. (I get so easily attached.) And to love a stranger as oneself implies the reverse: *to love oneself as a stranger.*

Divorced of its value in the real world, the typewriter had become art. There is hope in an afterlife for dead commodities, I say, softly, on certain mornings when I'm gargling at the base of the looking glass and I care to have a look. I'd like to live again as an object made for long pauses and deep breaths. I'd like to be vacuum-dried. Sometimes I have no idea where this is going, and this is one of those times. Our culture's public fascination with hoarding underscores our private fantasies of fusing ourselves with the objects we use and consume. An attempt to merge with machines, something which might make us forget our terminal flesh. To individualize machinery. When we are alone we become very lonely, though we find it frustrating to share our personal space with another person. We look, instead, for extensions of ourselves. An accessory that is not another person but an object. Sometimes people can turn into objects. Over time and with enough patience. See again: typewriter, which once designated the secretary who sat in place to press the keys. She didn't know it but she was becoming something else. She was forgetting about herself and the trauma of the body. The sadness of having one. The look I gave you when I knew you were looking (and I pretended not to notice

our own

retroprojections, a pause in the change of a frame, the unnatural emptiness of theaters). Unless we're the ones sitting here, waiting for the coming attractions.

it follows

listen, I'll satisfy you   we can
drape a curtain around
the plastic and call it glass and call this
a party   whatever you like or as you
wish   it's not something you can

say in a few lines   what is and what can be
done will be done or it won't
because we wouldn't
advance slowly   in little steps
you care to count   each split

in the sidewalk   childhood
fancies   a hole in the photograph that must
be me   the blurring at the edge
of a bush or shrub   that too is part
of the scenery   I preferred

to wait for you at home. You preferred to keep walking, advancing under a strobe and a receding Côte d'Azur skyline, reminding yourself to hold your finger here [record]. I'd like to think of you looking at the lights of Cannes and wanting to cry, or to be seen crying, which is even better, or worse. In plain view of an unseen audience and someone's cool command. Listen, it wasn't always like this. People coming and going as if lost backstage, interrupting other people's scenes and shouting out lines from scripts they'd picked up in wardrobe, three seasons ago. I no longer had any use for mirrors; my intention, instead: to form my face around the idea of other faces, other bodies; to look for myself in the mirror of others. As if every person could be broken down like the flesh from which we secure ourselves. It took practice and the kid had plenty, I'd recite, daily. Everything is doable under indeterminate conditions, the promise of hibiscus and two cubes of ice, a mason jar and the question of placement. I could and could not understand you. You understand that me telling you this is the best way I can think to really touch you or leave you with something of myself that you have also touched.

I imagined my new face
would better suit my age
and personality

the long slow delay
between a thought and
the expression   what I would

be today and not
tomorrow   there was something
exciting about to happen always

on the inside   so soon did I become
more tactile, elastic   more likely to
stand with just a hand

in my pocket
and less weight on one hip
on the street not knowing

anyone nor pretending to be
unable to withstand
the offers of strangers and

cheap freedom   nothing ever came
without a price in the world
I allowed myself

to enter caught
walking
like someone who

doesn't know
they were being filmed or
how to walk

I knew each and knew
even then what
to do with the tapes

I like snacks, small things, brief things, transitional moments, interludes. I like the eighties, the early nineties, the mid-two-thousands. The Zero Years. I like the future imperfect the most, more common in every other language than English. I like empty rooms, rooms with a view, backrooms; I like any room held behind a bookcase that doubles as a door in the stories I grew up with (the stories that sustain me). I like momentum. I don't like downtime. I like the meltdown. I like servitude. I like saying *yes* and I like accidents. I like thinking about each of your first days in your new lives in the United States of America. I like thinking about the morning you met in Lower Manhattan, and if it rained, and how the rain smelled.

A long unbroken shot of the seaport from a ferry vanishing in the distance, with seagulls flying overhead. I like dreaming in Spanish and singing happy birthday in Polish. I like phone calls from distant places, the static before a voice emerges, music and dancing. Sounds that are no longer with us. I like to sing, sometimes, in my studio apartment. I like headphones and train cars and eyeglasses and other private experiences. I like the beach, the sea, the feeling of salt on my skin when I swim. I like drifting even more; I like to veer, or wade, or skim the surface. But barely. I like the breeze, ecstatic fantasies that will never not ever drip from the screen. I like instant everything and I like to wait for it. I like movies, I like soundtracks, I like books, I like first pages a lot. I like the curve of his eyes and how they soften when I am looking. I like to pretend to not know when someone looks, and I like not wanting to know the reason why. I like seconds and thirds. I like doubles, duplicates, forgeries, rehearsals. I like diligence. I like to watch. I like listening.

and anyway what did either of us
know about duration or continuity?   I was born

in the city where
the cost of living exceeds the desire

to stay alive   the only death
I know of is not being seen

by others
I don't know what made me

think of this now, just as you turned
the music louder, just as I asked you to

tell me whose voice this is
rising like purple

petals in the vessel
of our body

the wizard

When I had been given my new teeth, and long after I had received my new eyes, it was determined that there was still more to do with a body like mine. On a Monday morning, before the snow fell, when the air was still cool and calm, I was brought into a small room with a single window, and placed down on a table. Unless I was asked to place myself down. This is the place, I remember thinking, where I will be introduced to my new sensorium. And so that I could retrieve the scene from the tomorrow of today, I opened my eyes wide very wide before clasping them shut, registering an internal click, as was my custom. The doctor, when he arrived, was firm but graceful, making sure to wish me a blessed new year before placing his palm down on my forehead, as if to anoint me, or to say good-bye to the me that I would leave behind. He was a specialist—they're all specialists, in one form or another—who very rarely came, I later learned, to this part of the city. Let's call him the wizard, with his long, curly brown hair, with his cold blue eyes, with his white gown that resembles an erstwhile cape. I could disclose further details; I could tell you what name he gave when he introduced himself but I'd rather invite your imagination; I'd rather ask you to ruminate on what kind of name might belong to a man who has his hair tied behind his neck in a bun, a man who uses aftershave against his cheeks, a man who speaks with a low rolling baritone in an accent that reminds me of a country to which I had never returned; a country where my mother was born, where to wish one a happy birthday is to sing their survival for one hundred more years. Sometimes it takes that long. To forget the trauma of dislocation, or the shock of arrival.

The film follows three children, the youngest of whom is emotionally withdrawn but gifted at playing video games, as they travel to California to compete in a video game tournament. I didn't get there till much later, when I was fully grown, when I had given up the idea of ever reuniting with my disappeared twin, or entering a video game competition, or singing (softly) "Send Me an Angel" by Real Life, in the pickup of a muscular truck, as seen from a roving dolly, desert sand kicking in the distance. I want to be tender but I also want to be merciless, an aerobics that undermines its actor's capacity to reason. What if I were to tell you about the babka presented to me, before I walked out the door of that small room with its single window, through the crowded lobby and down the single set of stairs, and re-emerged into the day that was slowly shifting toward dusk? The snow was still at least an hour away; sometimes I like to think in girth, and sometimes I like to think in time; distance is my specialty, if I have one, unless it's proximity; unless it's approximation. I could stand here, on the corner of M, and write these thoughts down, or I could begin walking, while continuing to write, the way I often believe that the prerequisite, if there ever were one, is movement, or the interval produced by a movement's delay. If I told you about my mother, and the way she pronounced her vowels, and the way she kept a photograph of her and her two sisters, before they'd escaped the small village one-hundred and six minutes (if one were driving) from Warsaw, the small village with only one road and the farm where all three of them had been born, and how the photo trembled despite its rigid borders, how the photo of all three of them—bundled blond angels huddled before a pear tree and what looks like wind coming in from the nearby river or stream but which certainly are scratches; technological errors or organic aesthetics, the passage from flesh to flesh—remained on her nightstand, secured in a single unmarked envelope, you would understand something about what I'd inherited besides a desire to receive this without the use of my hands. I could carry a lunchbox around to sate our hunger, or we could forage, instead, for a framework of translation that can only be uncovered between lines, or bodies, the point at which language stammers into ecstatic flight: murmurs that ask us only to feel and be felt, only to encounter without having to identify; to accept and enjoy that acknowledgement of unknowability, a dissimulation or disassimilation that resists conversion into lexical knowledge yet insists to be shared.

Blur as mobility. Blur, I often repeat (as if a mantra; as if entranced, drunk and engorged), as hospitality.

Scrolling can be a kind of choreography. Begin on the edge of your index. What do I know to be true? I remember asking, I remember being asked. Avenues run north and south. Streets run east and west. There was a time when I wished for death to come quickly, that I wished, rather, to disappear.

I know that we are going to cook the planet from the inside out. I know that all my memories of California intersect with memories of postapocalyptic landscapes (all of us orphans; all of us roller-skating strays), gathering at a point on the boardwalk where the mountains meet the sea. In light that we are living at the end of days, it's become harder to tell which is which, or when one becomes the other. Whatever I say is going to be something I remember from a movie, something I watched, something I felt desire from, a second-hand desire, which, maybe, is more real. Sometimes, without applause, I'll reminisce about the man in the white gown, and the way his eyeglasses dropped down on his nose, how he curled his consonants, when he asked me to be still very still but before he held up the mirror to my face, to show me what I've learned.

bloodsport

In my first few years of elementary school, I had a habit of stealing from the lost and found. I would look through the closet, knowing I hadn't lost anything, knowing, too, that I wanted to enter into the lives of the lost, the lives of the found: these strangers, now confidantes, whose memories were attached to their discarded or missing artifacts of experience. As if, when I held this grass plaid scarf, I could feel the neck enwrapped by it.

Today as we make our way north, I marvel at each sign promising or proposing a rest stop, which I sometimes imagine would offer me the hospitable pause to lay my own consciousness, finally and completely, to a temporary repose. If I couldn't just amputate my mind, then, for half the day. And what I wouldn't do with all the rest. Bedazzled by the local water treatment plant, as we pass another billboard cutting across the mirage of barren trees, I remember the story a student had told me, about the VR headset that can kill its user. I like my games like I like my everyday fantasies on the street, needing everything to be as real as possible, minus something unimaginable, so that it won't be real.

To make my memories correspond with facts, I search *VR headset that can kill its user* and thus complete the cycle of turning the anecdotal past into clickbait news. The idea of tying your real life to your virtual avatar has always fascinated me, says Palmer Luckey, the American entrepreneur and founder of Oculus VR, whose NerveGear device uses explosive charge modules designed to detect when the gamer has lost. You instantly raise the stakes to the maximum level and force people to fundamentally rethink how they interact with the virtual world and the players inside it.

At the urinals, I like to stand and watch the other players from the mirror as I wash my hands. I think you can tell a lot about a person by the way they handle themselves in moments of public abjection. The kind of stance they assume. Whether they place their left palm or their right palm on the tiled walls as they empty themselves, the sounds the body emits—a grunt or sigh? et cetera. I could convince myself that this, too, was part of my project, part of my research. That as I linger (leaning my weight on my right hip) at the open faucet and shake my palms until the flesh is as dry and worn as my jeans, I am infiltrating a zone of imaginative trespass. I wanted to know what went on inside of him. Inside of her. Isn't that how I became a reader? Isn't that how I remade my body into a tape deck, my eyes into a camera lens? I stand here, looking at the glossy surface specked with dust and bits of chemically enhanced animal meat, as if my reflected counterpart could return myself to another time, another body, as if looking itself were a kind of transport, remembering, as I looked, the chicken man of Philadelphia who said, as he continued to eat an entire rotisserie chicken each day for forty days, that he came to believe he could feel the pulse of the heart in my stomach.

I avoid meeting eyes with myself at the barber, as I am shaving my beard or while brushing my teeth. When it happens, and it seems so often to happen without my body's knowledge of its own mechanical movements, I feel disgusted.

There is an antique wooden dove perched near the narrow entrance of Geist im Glas, so perfectly does it fit inside the isthmus created by the cephalopod coat rack and the bar's curving countertop that I couldn't imagine it being anywhere else but here. Behind the bar, and the bartender's own face, is my own, caught once again unaware. Ghost in the glass. I close my eyes, hoping that when I reopen them, I'll have vanished, escaping with the understanding that I'll keep this spectral portrait in spite of my desire to drain and be drained, lodged between a shelf of nondescript liquor and six flowing taps, the way I keep everything, an image rimming a nearby patron's conversation about whether trees dream about their former lives as seeds, or miss the places from which their indigenous features derive.

I myself keep a detailed inventory of all the bodies I have read, and what ~~a confusing sensation it brings~~ confusion sensation brings. The little deaths do add up.

So in this scenario, I arrive at the lobby and walk out onto the Kurfürstendamm, watching, as I walk, the television tower visible from almost every block in the East as in the West, despite the body's relative distance from Alexanderplatz. I've done this every day for the three and a half weeks since I checked into my room on the fourth floor of the Hollywood Media Hotel, because I wanted to produce a memory, an image to be stuck in my mind when I would think of Berlin, forgetting for a moment what the image of the television tower would replace.

He was holding his penis like a cigarette. But no, that's not right. Many people hold their cigarettes in many different ways. And I don't even smoke. He was holding his penis, then, like a pool club. Gradients of fuchsia and magenta dominate every image that streams through my mind when I am like this; so up against the thrill of radical dislocation, unbroken immersion, that my eyes begin to flutter involuntarily and a smile, maybe, solidifies across my thick lips, the same satisfaction you get when you look back at your car after parking it.

I blink and I'm in Berlin again, picking up a local accent since the one I came here with is already impure. The week after new sex calls for another week of contemplation, and so it is, too, whenever I enter my notebook, the back of my head propped against this cheap cosmetic pillow for support, vintage static vibrating from a television I hadn't realized was on until now. In the interval (the shock of recognition), I receive an invitation to the Kumite, an illegal martial arts tournament in Hong Kong. Days later, after my Army superiors refuse to let me go, I will be "absent without leave"; I will say good-bye to my beloved sensei; I will leave for the Fragrant Harbour with its sparkling night-lights on the eastern Pearl River Delta. Unbeknownst to me, two Criminal Investigation Command agents (let's call them "Helmer" and "Rawlins") will be assigned to track me down and return me, energetically, to my proper place, whether their quarry is willing or unwilling. I click the remote and the screen turns dark. I could go back out and stroll the sprawling avenue of Western consumerism in the capital of the twentieth century; I could venture a visit to any of the numberless Nazi bunkers turned sex clubs turned private art galleries turned penthouses for their obscenely rich gallerists; I could browse a Reddit thread on the biggest debris hills in the world as I wait in line at Berghain; I could climb to the very top of the biggest debris hill in the world, and look down at the city undulating like a snake as I support my heaving body on the ruins of a CIA listening station, hoping, in my unfocused gaze, to make out my spotty form, laying there (laying here) with the window open in my unassuming room on the fourth floor of a Hollywood themed hotel in Charlottenburg, consoling themselves with such thoughts; I could second-hand shop (my lesser-known passion) at the German thrift chain I will later learn is an international criminal organization; I could draft an itinerary of things I would have liked to do this morning—when I write down where I have to go, what I have to do when I get to these places, I see so many things and people I would have never seen if it weren't for the list and the activities therein—I could flex my right thigh as I cross it over my left and absolve myself of any appointments but careless absorption in my notebook—have I ever really left?—I could investigate the DDR Museum, and survey all the photographs I've already seen before, looking at them until the schoolchildren's faces begin to resemble my mother's; I could do nothing but wait, nothing but nothing, until you install your apparition in the lobby; until the hotel manager rings at your avatar's request; until you sacrifice your body, too, for the calm belief in the warm and the familiar. Weren't we just making our way north? Weren't we just cataloging the variations of green in the Tiergarten's Rosengarten, its decorative gated entrance providing me with the fiction that this moment of prefab Hellenistic bliss was mine and mine alone? In a week, I'll be ~~somewhere else~~ someone else. The words drop in the midst of a muscle's murmur, just like that, a void that penetrates the body from within. And when I was in the men's room of this rest stop in the lower Hudson Valley, I wanted to be in Copenhagen, fondling the cool fins of the rusted bronze mermaid in a photograph. And when I was in Copenhagen, I wanted to be in Damascus, in London, in Kraków, in Siracusa, in Otranto, where I could convince myself that I had reached, on foot, the easternmost point in all of Italy. In Berlin, I ran my hand along every wall that remained, and prayed for the soundtrack of an afternoon storm. I awaited my big death scene.

from russia with love

What is something you expect to happen to you in the near future?

I am looking up, back against the cool blue bench, as we rise beside all the rooftops of buildings I've never seen from the ground. The F is nearly empty now, nearly always empty. When no one can tell who is smiling, and who frowns, underneath their mask. *What is something you expect to happen to you in the near future?* An advertisement for an airline I will not name here beams back at me as we move like a slingshot through the underground, as day bleeds into darkness, and we come out again, back into day. A man standing above me exits; when he pushes off the pole the imprint of his palm sticks, a balm of moisture I want to pocket, as if in the absence of touch, the absence of faces, we were each permitted to carry each other's residue around with us. I held him here, like this, for the necessary time of composition, when even I am not sure what my face looks like underneath the mask. And anyway, I am the only one here, a fact I won't register for several more minutes, when the train has stopped, when I've missed my stop, when the conductor's voice crackles against this thin strip of paper, the hurried scrawl of someone who fears time or maybe memory, and I'm asked to get off.

What is something you expect to happen to you in the near future?

I'll deplane. What a word. Deplane. And before I deplane, I'll fly, taking a route on the screen available against each seatback. How numinous. To be in the act while watching one's self do it. Isn't that what I've spent my whole life loving? Isn't that what I'm still—even now—in pursuit of? Intra-festum temporality: to desire proof of my own presence, which is to say, my own disappearance, the me that has always eluded me. The shape of my body will be an H, but lowercased, my hands folded across my lap, my knees bent, which is where the letter ends, where the letter always must end.

once upon a time in america

basically it is an adventure I am not really taking part in

basically a forty-hour prayer for the deliverance of my temptations

basically the blessedness of all small things and their caresses

basically an ode to unbearable urges such as these

and these
and these
and even more

the ones I've yet to be filled with

what is a poet
but a body
with the memory
of wind

what is a poem
but an image burned
in flesh the beauty
independent of the clothing

adornments, adulations

all I ask of this text

to be as close to
without reproducing
one single spring night

(an invitation subject
to repeating)
to recognize me without
having to look

to know this by heart
to unwrite or remain then
unwritten, one would become author
of a legend

blow-up

I wanted to be improvised and pliable. But I also want, I write, to be hard and memoryless.

When I was in my mid-twenties, and when others were already used to seeing me as someone who was being looked at for a living—a thing I still haven't gotten used to—some people said I was beginning to "blow up." Some people said that I was, right then and there (as if we paused the video and I was stuck, emotive but also motionless), in the midst of blowing or being blown, like a souvenir from the wind. Did they mean I was growing bigger by the minute, threatening to overtake my diminutive studio apartment, where I lived at the time of this blow-up (my first? my only), or did they mean that I was in danger of disappearance, of evaporating off the face of the earth? Or did they mean both of these things, since it takes both (desire/fear; exertion/surrender) in order to tell your story, to make it move with words.

camera buff

At my desk, or what serves as my desk, from which I taste and eat and play as well with words, I compose another memo to my future self while glancing, every other moment, at the postcards leaning against the window ledge, the immovable scenery of the nineteenth century blurring into the dead-end street that leads to a field for friends to meet, and beyond that, a cemetery.

I'd selected them, one by one, while traversing the arcades of Paris, or what was left of them, zigzagging an imaginary line through the fabled passages while on the trail of another exile. It seems, too, like a scene from another life, whenever I play the footage back, in wide shot from the lens of a companion's portable camera. Or maybe it's that I'm the outsider, an extra from another act who stumbled into this one, treading film from a moving picture that will never see the light of day. Each postcard told a story—the boy clad in a navy peacoat and matching cap saluting the viewer, as a blurred figure, taller, with his hands secured in both pants pockets, looks on against barren trees; the girl adorned all white, with a white ribbon atop her head, proudly propping her doll against her chest, as if it were a real baby, and the doll's identical wardrobe: white gown and white stockings and a white pair of flats; the confusion of subject and object, how the three women in the photo above are arranged, by height, in a staggered formation for the camera, how only one of them is without the wide-brimmed hat preferred by the other two, and how the walking stick seems to shoot out of the hatless woman's forearm, as she balances her body on its wooden shaft while sitting, the stone walls and marble angels, mid-flight and wingless, that surround the backdrop, as if they'd decided, the angels and the women, on a whim, to celebrate in the center of last century's ruins; they all were etched in sepia, so I had to imagine the colors—all the colors of the bricks set against the gray dawn, the bushes and trees, and the miniature eyes of the doll who looked out beyond the frame, never expecting anyone to return her gaze—yes, each postcard told a story, but also served as a kind of storyteller, witness to all the people who have ever looked upon them, all the places they'd been carried during their itinerant route, and this realization—that all our pictures don't just evoke memories, but create them; that all our photos, whether they ever really belonged to us, also belong to themselves, with memories of their own—made me revisit my own question to students, a prompt I often use during the first week of classes, about whether it's possible to miss a place you've never been, about whether it's possible to connect to your family's history, even though you weren't there, or whether trauma wasn't just cyclical but inherited, passed along like familial rituals and genetic code. Of what constitutes the "beginning" when what has been done has never been undone, and what's more, since the act of passage and break (detour, detainment) is still occurring.

If I had been under any illusions during that rainy afternoon in Paris, touring the arched-ceilinged arcades, an erstwhile labyrinth of commerce and entertainment, in the hopes of assembling my own Passagenwerk, I had by now realized that the holes in every photograph weren't an impasse but a legend signaling where and with what degree of pressure to further perforate the picture; to dive into the vacuum produced by the recording of light falling on surface, the inversion of the negative as a form of memory and experience, the devastation of time.

How to get out of the problem of naming? How to get out of the problem of creating art?

Sometimes, I remember writing, as I combed the letters, notebooks, photo albums, and journals that comprised my research, I wished that I had happened upon the records of my mother and father, too. What I wouldn't give to get closer to their internal reality, as they traversed borders unmistakable and invisible, as they became who they are to me: parents, and like all parents, strangers to their children. Sometimes I believe that these texts are my own parents' letters, that I've happened upon them here, and restored them, beside my own recordings, until the two—the past and the present, the East and the West—and the three of us, the three of our lives, became indecipherable, exchangeable.

dead poets society

My fists were in my pockets when I finally showed up and said hello. It was necessary to walk around the block twice before stepping in. I had to put on my face. I always have to put my face on before I step into a room. And I knew that I would know and not know so many other faces in this room. In the way that one can ever really know anyone.

In this room, or the garden outside, which is where we'd all be meeting. Meeting and reading and probably not listening, not really or not at all. All the faces and my own (still in the process of forming, because I sometimes get impatient. I sometimes can't wait for anyone. Not even myself). And here a garden without any flowers, without anything green at all except for a few spare dollars in a tip jar. (I hardly have enough to keep writing.) On a bar which housed all of those books, and all of those bottles of wine I still can't pronounce. A view of the park if you were standing so high. How I told it to you later.

All of these years and a poem is the only thing I've ever put in front of my face that I hadn't used to hide behind.

I was born this way, you think, and inside you know the feeling; you remember the feeling as though you're feeling it right now, because you've felt it so many times before. Like the moments where you were convinced you would live forever. The way time can drift and scatter and hold. All of it at once. And when you made yourself for the first time it felt as though your hips were on fire. Like you had burned yourself; the world and everyone in it.

And at times I even seemed to feel as if a stranger to myself.

But I wanted to find out what I am, so I take my hand and place it inside another's. I walk around and say all the right things, looking in all the right directions. Give all the right looks (though I can hardly remember which ones).

you looked and looked / and you could
wear your look like other people
wear their clothes / dispersing
your gaze as though your face were a hyperlink

(There was a lot of applause and some of it was real.)

And you think about temptation, about what really tempts me; about what really tempts you, I mean, when you are thinking of me. I could go on and on and on. We could go on and on like this until we gag.

And there are other times I will close my eyes in public, even in front of a crowd. And I can't get it out of myself, my self and the body that constrains it. And I can't get it out until I see it again, see it differently; until I reload the reel of film and align the projector and press play, or record.

Miami, a Sunday evening, late August. I know exactly when but to say it is to repeat it too closely, and I'd rather only see the moving images from afar; I'd rather only keep the vague semblance of my skin and sensation which I've committed to memory, altered, unfolded, and opened up.

(He was standing there in front of the casket and trying hard to keep his eyes from closing. Someone he knew and loved was lying there, or was meant to be. But the beloved wasn't there; he was no longer there, like an actor who replaces another halfway through the show without explanation, or applause. Everyone looks on and pretends not to notice, pretending never to notice a thing.

The man looked half-formed and frozen, somewhere between an object and a gesture. And the smell of a kitchen sink, the chemical lemon smell of something rubbed clean. His face didn't belong to him anymore. It was swollen and grotesque; it looked as though his face was coming loose from his suit jacket, the suit jacket a stranger had arranged over him, the white collar that girded it; his face, his neck, the swollen chin and cheeks. Like everything would spill over, onto the carpet, all the glossy leather and the flesh inside of it. And if it was thundering, he remembers thinking, it would.

And he stood there and tried hard to keep his eyes from closing. He shook his head as though he wanted it to fall out. He wanted to preserve all of it and none of it. To elevate, to cancel. To rub it clean but to rub it again. The stiff starched shirt, the half-closed casket that covered the legs, the cerulean tie that would never need to be knotted again. A wooden fan that made his eyes water more; that made his hair blow into his eyes and made the water stick. All of this to reflect what at the time he was trying so hard not to see.)

What I remembered most was the shaking. Standing and shaking and feeling as though he were abandoning another person so close to him; he felt as though he were abandoned too. Like a fact that will not change (not ever). And this is what he hated most.

And this is what I hated more than anything else I'd ever felt before, or pretended to feel.

But no, I don't want to keep looking right now.

It was better to let this drift and recede, fragments of a photo I would have liked to remain incomplete or uncompleted. Something you could fill in for yourself, and for me too. Yet thinking only of these fragments could bring me closer to myself, and by being further away I might even think to reach for it. I might even think to grasp it, deep down, bringing me deeper into myself than I had ever been before. Being alive all the time is a performance. Being alone is like watching another.

(I'd had that dream that everyone has and I kept having it. I'd wake up and walk outside and sit down on the subway or maybe I'd stand, not noticing the fact that I'd forgotten to wear clothes until I looked in the mirror after a bathroom break, sometime between classes. Sometime between nine and noon, or maybe just after, maybe one o'clock or one-fifteen. I'd look up as I rubbed the tips of my fingers together and shook my palms dry and I'd look down and I'd realize it was true. My flesh still damp and dripping. I'd wake up in sweat. I always awake in sweat. Someone tomorrow will ask me whether it is really a nightmare or whether it isn't a fantasy.)

I like to keep photographs of everything
I see inside of me and so I
thought I might pull the skin back and peel it off

the soft, thin layer and then the hard stuff / the stuff
that seems indescribably detailed and incomprehensible
all at once / it doesn't really take much / that I might have

a look inside / and I would try to show you
with words / why I ever wrote anything in
the first place and before / it was written it would

always be here anyway
I said, didn't I
that I wanted to know what I am

the secret of my success

Of their lives in North America when they'd arrived or their life in New York City when they'd finally met, as if both bodies had flowed into one single stream, river of kite and cut ribbon, I can't say, except that they had at least one child, a son who changed jobs as if they were a pair of pants; I could never tell if he was always working or never working, so easily did he seem to slip into the role required of him, until he had become, in no short order, a reporter and an actor, bartender and waiter, instructor, translator, media artist, model, and—the role that seemed to gather them all, or to make each distant filament cohere—a student, and I often thought, whenever his name appeared and I returned, with no will of my own, to our original encounter, before all of this, when he was just a boy, and he parted his hair, like all the other small boys, after his father, that there was a great deal that must have been given up, a great deal he had to give up for the character, always exchanging one accent for another, so to speak, as his own voice began to fade, the performance one at a time and each time beginning to chip away at whatever was inside of him, I can't say for sure—she went on, and I wished, in spite of my growing interest in her stories, that she'd relinquish the task of telling them, since we were here, the two of us, to serve other purposes, and it was my own task—wasn't it? I had already been paid in full—to ensure that she could stay still very still long enough for the flash to erupt from my camera's eye, an improbable aspiration if she were to continue moving her lips, and gesturing, too, with her hands as she talked, as she was talking now.

Later, although I'm not sure when, she returned, as I adjusted my exposure, he was already moving throughout Europe, inching, if he were following his mother's trajectory, in the reverse, moving east until he arrived in Berlin. And as he moved, he read the correspondences of those who had also been put in motion, from east to west or west to east, and he wrote back to them, too, since the point of a letter isn't transmission, but imminence—something he said once, and even explained in one of the letters—the staged proximity of the addressee who is only ever at hand. I ask myself what did he do with all those letters, all those missives to people who were already dead or missing—

what dreams may come

I was born just after the end of the war. I never went to school; my parents arranged for me to have private lessons. I can, you can see, write my name. Before I was born, my mother worked as an opera singer at the Semperoper, and it was here that I first learned how to smile. It's not a stretch to say I enjoy wearing the clothes and jewelry that my mother left for me after she passed. Each day I am someone different, sometimes a queen, sometimes a bishop, sometimes a policeman or the Pope, sometimes Luise of Prussia. But I don't tell everyone that. Today though, on the day of this interview, I am Luise von Roth.

The note stopped there, and I couldn't tell, I couldn't be sure whether what was being described was from an actual letter or an extract from a story, or whether it made any difference, since I had come upon the paper not far from the Dresden opera described therein, and so whether it was nonfiction or fiction had little bearing to me, who had now entered the story, as either Luise von Roth or the Pope, or neither of them, as maybe the interviewer, then, or the sound engineer that would later graft the audio on the video track, and rework the pauses and the delays, since the letter had also mentioned the difficulty of articulating words clearly, on account of a birth defect, in a place of nativity in which the person speaking was considered "mentally impaired," although I'd omitted that detail, as well as several others. It's always a matter of deciding what to salvage and what to let drift into the ether, hoping, either way, that what is gone will never vanish for good, and that everything, everything, eventually resurfaces, in one format or another.

When we were still learning to be human and tender to one another, I told myself that I would one day become a great reader. Most people, I think, possess grand dreams of writing page after page and book after book, but what I wanted, ever since, I think, I first learned to read, was to read as many books as I could in the little time provided, knowing too well that there's a great many books in the world and a great many of them will soon disappear, as if they'd never been written in the first place, as if their authors, too, were not even ghosts but persons who had never lived.

In Dusseldorf, where I walked along the parade of twinkling lights, the miniature red huts bisected by rows and rows of miniature Christmas trees, the open-air vendors and pretzel tents—shaped in the symmetrical knots of the baked bread for sale, rolled in cinnamon and sugar or doused in a coarse mustard, an earthy color, like wet sand—that signaled the start of the winter market, I rediscovered an old pastime from childhood, a game in which I played the role, here in my double-breasted black peacoat, my black jeans, my mustache and gray scarf, of spy, someone who is always playing someone else, like a matryoshka doll, where each layer reveals only imitation, another mask beyond this one, and beyond this one, another … and here, as if still in disguise, I slide into other crowds, in other cities, in rain-slicked Tokyo against the flood of taxicabs and Sardinia at dawn to retrace the steep incline from the docks by heart, in Bologna, under the numberless archways, of where I've walked and where I've read or watched others do the same, *where cherry blossoms blow loose from trees and ride the rendered wind.* When I enter the crowded tavern, I will always ask the bartender for a taste; I ask what they like to drink, what they like to eat, and how the dashi is prepared. I never shed the curiosity of a three year old and sometimes I convince myself that it's been my greatest gift as a reader, since any reader, just like any writer, deals in the currency of desire, solicitation of the voyeur whose gaze wants to be returned.

It didn't surprise me, for instance, that when I finally did make it to Poland, in a village so close to Berlin that only decades before it was considered Germany—borders being nothing but arbitrary and artificial—I had the realization that I could have just as easily been born here, in this port city near the drift of the Oder, erstwhile capital of Pomerania, original member of the transnational Hanseatic League—at the time more powerful, much more powerful than any kingdom, let alone any concept of a nation-state—in a place that was, in reality, several hundred kilometers from the birthplace of my mother, a place she had never been, would never go, if and when she returns to Poland. My mother's mother—I, who knew only enough English to ask of me: "you be good boy," during our regular visits each weekend, found work, when my mother and her sisters arrived, as a factory worker, assembling countless tubes of toothpaste in the deserted industrial zone of nearby Long Island City. My father's father—just like my dad, another J—worked for a North American toothpaste company, and it was because of this connection to the United States that he was granted permission to leave Cuba, a kind of permission to flee that had nothing to do with consent, nothing to do with choice.

And so some part of me believed that if they didn't meet as family—my abuelo and babcia, before they were ever called those names—they would have met as colleagues, accomplices in the double labor of unincorporated wage work and assimilation, underbelly of democratic capitalism in this new state of self-made men, absorbed by men and women for whom the state had all but ignored or outcasted; they would have met through a shared sense of care, I think, as a mode of survival, held together like the plastic laminate that secured the toothpaste assembled by I, who I seldom think about anymore, and so I sometimes feel as if I need to write about her life—all the things she did or might have done, all the people she'd still become—so as to have an excuse to write *to* her, which is to say, to think about her again. I know, or have long held the suspicion, that most of us think to write, but the kind of writing I'm after is what happens inside our heads when we write to think, to form thoughts, understanding that anything remains inert unless and until we decide to pay attention, to animate it, as one holds one's breath to give back life to another. Sometimes I think that all writing—all reading—is a space for the back of the mind to come forward, and that we often have to repeat the act as a daily practice, that we need to continue to teach ourselves to hear, and see, and remember the world all around us, to remember what it's like to be in our bodies at moments such as these.

powder

—and as she said this, her face seemed to freeze, as if I were no longer the photographer or director but the one watching, and the video lagged long enough to insert myself into the shot in her place, without ever considering who it was that would release the shutter, after all. But as soon as this fantasy scenario shimmered before me, so her face, too, became reanimated, and the only photo produced amidst the facial shifts and muscular contractions that presupposed the enunciation of other details—the son's first morning in Berlin and the stumbling stones he'd helped brush clean, the cinematic hotel with its winding staircases and red carpeted hallways in the heart of Charlottenburg, the keycard that had the mysterious quality of unlocking all other doors; he says words, she said, English words, as if he's hearing the music for the first time as it's coming out of his body—other details, as I said, which I do not wish to relate here, was a portrait smothered in blur and darkened by the lack of light, since the sun had changed positions in the sky, or the sky itself had changed its settings, from the color of my jeans to a metallic gray, and it reminded me (the sky and her face, after it had been developed) of the story about a lab assistant whose body had transitioned into a photographic plate, with pale flesh that photographed as navy in strong light, and, at twilight, as a kind of powder, effervescent, barely-there, on account of the body absorbing so much silver. If there was a moral to this story, it had been lost on me, except for the dangers of the workplace, the hidden cost of our daily labor, or maybe the sacrifice of what it takes to turn someone into an object; that sometimes, after enough attempts, the obligatory technique of the artist is to merge, finally and absolutely, with their art.

batteries not included

The wind will never stop this year.

This year and the one before, and probably the one that comes after. The one after the one that comes after. Anymore, any longer. The wind won't stop. And as I pull myself inside (for cover), L's text comes in to remind me about all the flights we still need to book. I wonder if the wind will take me. I wonder if the wind will take me and how far, or when. Sicily in June. Brooklyn in July. Berlin in August. And how far back I need to go to get here. As a child, unlike any other child, I never wanted to fly. As a thirty-three year old (thirty-three-years-and-three-days), it is all I ever want, or all I'll ever want. Sometimes I forget which.

♦

I'm meant to list five things I know to be true, five things I know to be not true. I wonder if you can tell the difference. And if you can't, can I?

♦

I will never pay for a window seat again. L texts back, saying that's fine, saying she'd rather have the view, if she can have it and she can.

♦

What is it that keeps you up at night?

♦

The sudden ejection from a plane while traversing the clouds. Some things don't come to life until you write them. But writing—doesn't it?—always prefigures a form of death.

♦

I forgot how to smile on command. (This I write to myself.) And I know because I study the photos the way Marilyn Monroe did; I study the photos not to see what's wrong but whether anything comes off right.

♦

I've outgrown my position, she said, turning to me in Happy Baby, as I picture this notebook, and wonder where we are going next. What it pretends to show or does it.

♦

Death always comes softly.

♦

I like to look at other people as if they're already dead. It helps me look closer.

♦

Movies help me learn English, J said. I was sitting in his arms, sitting or just lying there, the length of me cradled in his arms. And in my memory, we are watching *Batteries Not Included.* S will walk into the parlor in a moment, or in two moments (however long it takes for a moment to pass), and she will take me from my father and place me on her lap and raise my arms to the ceiling, to the sky, as a pair of spaceships enters the apartment, stage left, through the window left ajar.

♦

Everything that is broken can be fixed. (This is the lesson of the movies. Or at least my first lesson, the first lesson I can remember.)

♦

There's a choice to memory, L says.

I text back: Sometimes your memory chooses for you.

♦

The two alien spaceships are dubbed "The Fix-Its" by the town because of their knack for repairing broken things.

♦

Or is it that everything that is fixed *is* ruptured, damaged for the fact of the fixing.

♦

What did you do last night?

I am meant to respond. I am given a set of questions from which to respond. What did you do last night? I sat next to a fishbowl and ate a forty-two-dollar steak—forty-two dollars, he repeated, before tax. Inside the fishbowl was the Statue of Liberty in miniature, and one fish swirling under and around its vacant torch.

♦

Pretend, I mean. Not show. I know—or know that I feel—I am showing you everything.

♦

To be fixed—you will remember—is to be immobile, stationary; to be securely placed or fastened. To crystallize in a final form.

♦

I will use everything, even the parts I don't want to use; even the parts that aren't mine.

♦

My mom warned me about the ways I could poke my eyes out. I can still hear her voice calling from the kitchen, or feel my eyes inside my skull, and if I could see anything I'd see her face. The soft green-brown eyes. But I need to linger here, or else I'll forget it. But I need to move on, or else I'll forget it.

♦

Some things take time to happen. Some things bear repeating. Some things come back and some things we will never return to. I promise

I will be better organized next time.

♦

A tax also means a heavy demand.

Or, obsolete: to enter a name in a list.

♦

I never know how this will end.

That's why—I often think—I go; that's why I keep going.

♦

A friend says she went to Kate Millet's funeral this year. Just to see what it was like.

♦

No difference between desire and disgust, I often think, when I'm done with whatever it was I was fixing my concentration on.

♦

Does one require a rotating screen—a rotating series of screens—for one to have their biography assembled? Do all biographies require full disclosure, or do they require narrative void?

♦

Pretending an author is queer while reading them instantly makes their writing more readable.

Don't believe me, A asks, without the question mark. Try Norman Mailer.

♦

MM's female corporeality—her bodily-bigness, and its expansive reach—was a threat to national order.

♦

If one were to add a third M we would be reading our own satisfaction.

♦

Is it better to be felt or to be reached for?

♦

Flesh impact is rare, B would later say. Flesh that photographs like flesh. You feel you can reach out and touch it.

♦

Eyes the color of information. Eyes the color of data being read and retrieved for later. (An archive of eyes.)

Women on street corners with their eyes closed.

♦

Sometimes the something that makes you a star is the same thing that might subvert the whole constellation.

♦

If I accumulated observations of the real and recollections of a dream, recollections of a dream and images from memory, would either of us pretend to be able to know the difference?

♦

How quick it seems when I'm beside you—

One friend says to another on a train racing through the German countryside, one black and white hand on top of the other.

♦

What I want—what I always want—is to write about A Possible

X, as if X is permanently attached to a state of futurity, waiting to see what X might still become; waiting to see what is endlessly approaching from the edge of the frame.

♦

I've already forgotten who is asking the questions and who is answering them.

♦

In this and all scenarios, I am X.

♦

(This list was originally smaller.)

♦

To enter a scene without disclosing any of the details is also to suggest that you are the one responsible for everything that occurs on just the other side of the page. The burst of orange on a cheek, the swinging latch of a door sliding back, the smell of the wind on one's face. To write mood is to return me where I belong, which is inside you.

♦

By the time the two alien spaceships give birth to three baby alien spaceships, M and M grow closer; the first M finds the other M's paintings beautiful, which makes the second M feel better about their art, and to not give up on it.

♦

I always think that art is the one thing I won't give up on, even if my body gives up first.

♦

S and J had to become something other than aliens before they had their two babies, one of which was me.

♦

(To X something is to cross it out, to nullify it, to show that it is wrong or not wanted, to make it void.)

♦

And in reaching for something one must reach more than once.

♦

Any excavation of a body is a withdrawal but also an advancement. It is as if we are loaning this body on credit. It is as if we are loving this body on credit.

♦

(There is something of the body that cannot be contained in a photograph or a caption. There is something of the body that cannot be represented in text. I am thinking now of control, or its utter absence.)

♦

And in the iteration of reach is the amplitude of lack.

♦

Is it true or isn't it that I only ever write about my own disappearance.

♦

But could it also be that X marks the spot? In another movie, in another life, there's a map being unrolled slowly as the camera moves from mid-shot to close-up. Faces gather round as if at a funeral.

Another way of saying this is *this*
must be the place.

dirty dancing

At the dentist I am lying on the table, as is so often the case, with my mouth held open by a woman whose face I can't see but whose voice I continue to hear—that's it, sweetie, that's great, just a little while longer—as a man to her left jams an instrument against my gums and continues drilling. I am, I might as well admit, a curious person. I don't ask about the material being fused onto my dead teeth, I don't ask about the instrument with which the man drills, or the man's name, or where he lives, or what he thinks of my smile, or whether he is circumcised, or how long he's been doing this for, or what he is doing, what we are all three of us doing here, not because I can't talk (I can't) but because I'd prefer not to know, to hold this lack of knowledge like any secret as the gloved hand (anonymous) moves in and out of my mouth, in and out of my mouth, an anesthetized oral penetration I've often found dirty, even as a child, lying there (just as I am lying here, without a sugar free lollipop reward), the smell of latex and the sound of fingers probing me in ways I cannot see and will never understand, probing me in ways I want to keep secret, if only so I can write about it later, to externalize my dental erotics and let it leak against this thin sheet of paper, the way I'm dribbling saliva, right now, from each corner of my lips.

exit through the gift shop

A feeling I've had before, at least in dreams, and I know it. How horrible, this particular sensation of unraveling. As if I'm melting into the pavement except just my mouth is failing, my immovable lips. I feel each tooth slide out from the gums before the blood rushes in, wanting to scream, wanting to confess, to cry out for help—mama, mama, mama—nothing comes, except a kind of indistinct hum; nothing comes, except blood, more blood carrying my teeth in its briny flow. I let myself lie there, in the middle of day that looks like night. In the middle of the street that looks like a stage. With my head down. Resigned to silence and having no mouth at all from which to say anything, if I'd wanted to, if I even felt I could. They say you get bad dreams. From eating so much red meat.

It's not that I'm shocked by my death but by the way it happens. An inaudible death. A drawn-out death that doesn't make a single sound. And I recalled other dreams; what appears to be a bathtub filled with blood is in fact rose petals. And when I look back in my bedroom there are admirer notes scattered across the mattress and the nightstand and the polished wooden drawers. As I open the closet door, a roll of photos taped to the inside dangles out, falling like water from the faucet. Private photos, images that didn't exist for the public. Outtakes of driver's licenses, for instance, government-issued IDs, faculty passes, my VIP customer credentials at Video City. All the photos shot before a security desk's impassive surveillance. I had never seen these photos myself, which is to say, I had never seen how I looked when I thought no one was looking, and so I looked upon each picture with a sense, first, of wonder, and eventually, with dread. What was being documented was not my person but the production of my documentation; the photos were objects, and the objects, as I continued to browse the flimsy plastic squares, were their own traces.

And later—unless this part comes first—my head and body sprouting from the same pipe or hole I'd just exited. Dismayed, to be covered in all that shit, knowing class was about to begin, and that I was on my way and late again. I tell you this because in my dream I spoke to you very clearly and without hesitation about this recent experience; always confusing dreams for memories, and thinking it was incredible I had never told you about my ordeal in the tunnel and the landfill and the shit in which I'd bathed. Given we have become so close.

I like the privacy of hotels but I also like to go outside my room—the stairwell, the lobby, the café that turns into a dazzling chop-house at night—to read. I like to read here because of the secrets that all provisional spaces harbor, the way a hotel's rotating doors and circuitous hallways invite their guests to make certain adjustments to their inner selves, which have transformative qualities, of course, for the world of language and speech. I remember mentioning this to a mother, a woman who was near death. As it happens, the author and I are often interchangeable. As it happens, it was not the first time I'd sampled the elegant, dry spirit distilled from the aromatic resin of the Mastiha tree, a gnarled and twisted evergreen found clutching the hillsides of Chios, but it was the first time I'd enjoyed this sumptuous digestif in the company of people whose names I could only conjure through speculation.

Today my father played a merchant who dealt in misplaced things. Notes toward my first monograph were among them. He'd found a folder ... several stacks of folders bound together with makeshift twine, and he'd begun selling these indistinct jottings on the market, which was open, like so many things in those days, to the theater of the public, and as such, it was not long before I counted myself among the curious faces hovering over the carefully displayed merchandise, my own memoranda looking back at me, my own unrehearsed thoughts and the prices they each fetched. It's worth putting down. But there were other encounters, of course, misadventures at port and delayed trains, spy games in Dubai, recruited by two men I'd only seen before on CCTV. Willfully exploited (for the fun of it). One trick involves placing down my face as if to make a fingerprint (a face print) in a sort of catalog. My face, each time, comes back differently. And if I do it just for the novelty (just for a good time), I am required to manipulate my countenance by forceful impression, rubbing vigorously the flesh and tugging my hair, too—so strenuous was this activity and such pressure exerted on my scalp I'd be bald before long—to return to my old appearance (in the mirror), I often feel as if a part of me is still there, still here, spread across miscellaneous times and spaces, variable modes of consciousness, identity split and prismed, the way we watch the sky at night, misplacing a floating aircraft for a nameless star. Because I so often relied on fantasy and the likelihood of scenario, I myself have been, for the greater part of my life, entangled. I remember the hollow echo pulsing behind or below me, as if I were in a tunnel, or, although I'd never considered this until now, as if I were the tunnel, a channel of the body with all of its pathways and arteries trafficking the mystery of ourselves, or inviting the unknown volume of the soul to spew.

It didn't have the quality of a remembered sound or one reaching you from the inside. And I remember when, during a seminar on *failed media*, if ever there were such a thing, failure, I mean, without meaning, a lesson I'd given on the glossograph, a small device that was to be placed in the mouth to reproduce speech on paper, introduced in the 1880s and already abandoned by the turn of the century, on account of the inability of a machine to reproduce consciousness, and the general reluctance to think when offered the alibi of mechanical friction, so that hardly any evidence remains of its existence, excepts perhaps these spare pages. And just as soon as I retrieved the memory of the glossograph or its swift annihilation, I also returned to one of the numberless Nazi bunkers I toured while in Berlin, where I viewed, among other curiosities, the iridescent 3-D scans of dead animals, supermarket roadkill revived by the artist not as a form of resurrection so much as a reminder of their souls, since meat-eaters, I myself among them, hardly ever consider the fact that what's on our plate is an animal who once died, which is to say, an animal who once lived. I think what the artist was doing was not extracting objects from souls but extracting souls from objects. And then I remembered other things, the design objects of "poultry" and "beef" lasered at some factory and later lathered with oil and syrupy cornstarched barbecue sauce for presentation on my flimsy dining tray during transatlantic flights, but also the failure of flight, terror of eruption or evacuation, Air France Flight 447, intended for Paris, leaving from Rio de Janeiro, which went down hours after takeoff. I read somewhere, I remember reading, that the first passenger they found was still strapped in his seat, floating in the middle of the Atlantic Ocean, his boarding pass still tucked neatly into his collared shirt pocket.

Am I still in the dream? Are we still dreaming? I looked through hours and hours of footage, another artist told me, when we were each of us back in the city, fingering olives at a literary salon somewhere in Tribeca, as he described his meticulous process of isolating each fragment before re-creating it as a grainy, distorted still. I was looking, he'd said, for something that I felt was true. You know? You need some element of truth to the image, because when you pause the tape, something happens. This kind of pathos enters them, a narrative that perhaps isn't there when you're watching in real time. And as we talked, fingering our olives within the triangle (more accurately a quadrilateral) below Canal Street as it continued to rain, I thought, too, about my own tapes—this collection of VHS, and how the story itself morphs, how the story expands, just by slowing down the footage, for instance, just by rewinding again and again and again, knowing that repetition never follows the laws of exactitude, and when I take a photo of this screen, just now, and spread it across twenty-four by thirty-six, I make sure to first zoom in, to crop the rest, so that details that were barely visible, hardly there, emerge on the surface as the primary subject. And so it often seems that time passes in at least two different streams: reality, which was open to all, and the reality of the self, which was imbued with a kind of potency that wouldn't have been possible out in public, and rather, had to be found, between the lines as one says, a kind of internal registry that can only be excerpted, opened up, drawn out, annotated.

let the right one in [returned as a body]

To measure the circulation within my brain, G places a transducer to my face, to the flesh above my ear. I like the part before—G's gloved hand applying a cool gel to my neck, my scalp, my eyelids—the best. Later, the instrument sends out a message to my brain, which my brain will or will not send back. When the energy reflects, the monitor to my left graphs the unit into colors, each hue (I guess) designating a different intensity. Sound turns into pictures, pictures turn into speed, when speed can be made material, returned as a body. Even if I couldn't look, as I'm looking now, I can hear it—the sound of waves breaking, or the beating of wings—collaborative incantation of the outside-inside, when the moment of coincidence turns into song. Waves on the shore, the flight of angels, or birds. Unless it's the swift ejection of a bomb, the long, slow descent. I want to keep it inside so I say nothing, except to ask about the name, to know the name of the instrument that makes art out of unseen breaths.

raiders of the lost ark

Now the sun was setting. Now the sun was coming up. Approaching, almost here, on the edge of it, like all the best things in this life.

It's only when I am in motion that I feel free, or free enough to be alone with myself, the way I never am. Portland's streets are empty at this hour, too, cleaner at this hour or all the time, the other end of the world from the blistering sound of rubber and the smell of gas and trash burning in Brooklyn, where a tree grows, alongside so many others, even in the evenings, when it's too dark to count the seeded statues and their outstretched boughs as I run beside them. And when I replay the scene, it comes out like *Trainspotting*, Iggy Pop blaring in the background; herd through the walls, the way the best movie at the cinema is the one seeping in from all the adjacent auditoriums, reassembling a one-of-a-kind copy. I'm remembering this from memory, which is another kind of translation. A week from now, I remember thinking, there'll be something good enough to write down. So I started writing. A week ago, I'm still grazing knees with E in the backlit brilliant of my mobile's notes. Everything already in motion, remember? The way that a life was lived so it could be written, I mean heard. And it takes so much, and it takes so many of us to really listen. And what's important isn't an audience—not you, despite how much I cherish every reader; not even E, with whom I'm writing, to whom I'm lending my voice—but the inscription, the act of inscribing, which turns facts into actuality. And so I remember to sign the date at the very top, because I know a timestamp is a benediction and a prayer. But for what? Only more prayers.

The point, I know, is to keep moving, whether it's "Lust for Life" in the background or just the whoosh of my mind when it empties out, the way a drain unclogs after a momentary pause, to take everything in. What I really like is what is different from me. Maybe that's why I fell in love with books, fell in love with reading about all the places I would never go, could never go, only so I could imagine all the people I would have liked to meet. I love anything so long as it demands endurance, so long that it endures in its uncertain impermanence. Being human is an art, too, and the greatest one.

E and C, he and I, me and you, each of us were born interlopers. It's what's made us who we are, even if we didn't have a choice, even if we never exactly got to choose. The way that when I finally got to Cannes, all those years ago, he was leaving, forcibly escorted from the premises amidst all the hoopla of Hollywood as it makes its annual trip to the Riviera. The way the two of us looked at each other with our own shit-eating grins, wondering, silently, *What the fuck is this guy doing here?*—understanding, without having to understand, that we were each asking ourselves the same thing.

a history of violence

Excuse me sir—have you got the time?

The man was hard of hearing, so I thought, until I asked again. I haven't got a watch. Except he said, *I haven't got to watch.*

Which was true, because he had on sunglasses, and only then—after I repeated my request—did I realize he was blind, or partially blind, the kind of blindness that maybe all of us experience later in life, later or very early, before our eyes really adjust to being in our bodies.

He looked sixty, or maybe sixty-five. I'm never good with ages, and most people think I'm much younger than what my driver's license says, which is DOB: 4-17-1985. Which makes me thirty.

He must have seen me staring, seen me or sensed me, because he took off his sunglasses and started sucking saliva, preparing to spit. Being inside here made me comfortable, even with all the shaking and the babies crying. I know, it's strange to admit a thing like that but I am, I've often been told, a strange person; I, too, had inferred my queerness at such an early age, and as I got older, it only got closer to my heart.

He put his sunglasses back on and I read the time on his watch, which was digital. I always confuse the little hand with the big hand: which means what, what amounts to when, and now I didn't have to tell; the time told me.

I breathed a satisfied sigh and took my phone out, to try and write whatever it was I was thinking or feeling before it escaped me, something I'd only remember in passing or passage, on the F or waiting for one below the cobblestone streets of downtown Brooklyn and unthinking, which is when the best thinking occurs.

I like walking through life like this, time on my hands or in my hands, though hardly ever on my wrist, not like that, not exactly or not at all; nothing to do but to do it, and my whole life to do it. I'm desperate. I hope I never lose it.

♦

He's not old but not young, and he never takes sugar with his coffee, or even milk, and definitely not cream. He likes the work of the Latin American Surrealists, and the French Existentialists, and the Expat Modernists, and the German Expressionists (post- and pre-war), and the Italian Neorealists, and the English Metaphysical Poets—although he's only really read one—and more than anything, he likes the Situationists, who mostly published pamphlets, Q&As and rules about sidewalk etiquette or how to walk through a city on a curve. He likes sex and especially the smell of it. You can picture him in Brooklyn Bridge Park, running shirtless or with an orange tank top and blue mesh shorts or black nylon stretch pants, curving a line through Brooklyn Heights into Dumbo, running along the cobblestones and counting each barely-there crack in the sidewalk (or at the entrance to Pier 9, the last drips of vanilla ice cream on his chin, a neon volleyball at his feet or in his hands—why not?—since we're painting pictures) with his eyes shut and a strange expression on his face, as if he could feel each second and he was savoring it.

It's a promising scene, especially when viewed from a bridge. Add some music, a little concerto by The Human League, maybe Prince, the earlier stuff, *1999* or *Dirty Mind*—albums so good you can pick just about anything—add a slow-motion pull-back panorama, and you've got a real stunner. Something good enough to make us sob.

He stops walking when he hits the cinema on Court Street; the marquee above his head with the names of each film in black, half the letters missing or absent. Three guys and a girl, in their twenties, mindless and prepared to die in any old alleyway.

It's that, or a movie about an orgy of witches. Everything else already started. Looking from his phone and the synopsis to the sign and the signatures, missing or absent, left and right, up and down, like an aerobics infomercial, until he stops looking and walks in.

♦

Do you remember that? I don't know where it came from, just now, or even at all, but I remember being on the train together and I even remember the sound of the conductor—an automated machine after all, always the same announcement, more or less—and we had been so afraid lately, so full of fear the way I never am or the way I never can admit. So much of life is a show and I was showing you how vulnerable and insecure I could be, how much I doubted myself, who I was, or who I'd become, or who I'd meant to be, the way when we look at old journals, old notes written on napkins we'd forgotten to discard, old emails, old post-its, missing letters, missing or absent, letters never sent out of fear or uncertainty or both, anecdotes and annotations, messages written in margins, collage, coda, and epitaph, we don't remember who that person was though we recognize the hand that wrote it as our own.

I was worn; I was wearing down. Maybe that's why I so very often wear so little. Afraid of the enormity of objects, their absentminded immortality.

I had an idea that I could cut into reality, in private and in public, guillotine it and rearrange the splinters. The costs keep rising, for an idea like that, in a place like the one I've placed myself. My choice, of course, to live like this, to be so hungry, all the time, to never be sated, could I even know?

Art should be a bullet; the role of the artist is to take the shot.

Each day I felt better, or different, which isn't the same thing but seemed like it to me, for the simple fact that difference meant I was changing, and the worst thing in the world is to be static, which isn't the same thing as being still.

The train kept rocking until we became one person, clutching each other from each other's waists, me balancing my back against the steel as we hurtled on, the train and our lives, underground then above it then back below, from a vacuum that reminded me of space, or my idea of space: vast, dark, mostly silent except for the occasional *whoosh* (a star exploding, or being born) to a balmy March morning, sun-caked windows, a passing tree, a passing steel giant, another tree, unless I'm the one passing, letting my eyes drop or trying to between stops and opening them to see yours, green like my own except all the way and I've only ever been in between my whole life, my eyes and everything else. I don't know why I'm telling you this, or why it occurs to me now, the image and the sound and even the smells (rust, metal, rain, coffee, barbecued meat wrapped in pita in the hands of someone sitting below me, and the hands themselves: the soft damp flesh smell I look for everywhere) aligning in my mind like a reel of film placed over the one that should be playing, any other moment except this one. I held your hand until your hand disappeared.

And then I saw the time I died in Greenpoint, before and also after, for an editorial that would later surface in Paris, in expensive magazine shops, overpriced collectibles, purveyors of coffee table pastiche.

In the photograph, you can see my face through my killer's legs: wide, outspread, flourishing her high heels and pointed calves and her pistol, which you wouldn't see if it weren't for the shadow of the gun created on the wall where my torso props, one knee bent, each arm out to protest the inevitable. The room is dark and my head is lit from above, a black and white freeze frame in which my silhouette is surrounded by a sort of halo: saint and victim all at once, which seems natural, a normalized custom—confession, death, and the canon, one after the other, out with a shot and a sanctification, and it was the best thing I could ever hope for, in this life or in the one created by the photographer and the lighting crew, and the art director, and the reader, too, if we can call them readers, whoever paid 45 euro for a copy of the glossy issue of *Flaunt* nine months later and five years ago.

Every act of creation presupposes an act of death, like a paper negative, and writing is about slaughter as much as it is about sustaining life. At least that's how I always figured it, how I'm figuring it now, you looking at me with something I can't name, something I can never name, since any moment reinscribed by the writing act destroys that moment, (re)dresses it with an altered glaze: an imprint that clarifies the existence of the real thing, unless it replaces it.

The real thing, and the rarest. That's what I wanted; that's what I always want, in fact and in fiction.

But it wasn't your beauty itself that I admired; it wasn't your ass or your eyes, or anything that you could see if you were looking too; it was a side of you that I've gradually come to know and will probably never know completely. And yet I know it well enough to try and kill it.

Maybe I'm only saying it that way because I really believe it or because I think it sounds good, on paper or against your lips, or maybe it's only that I've been listening to Broken Social Scene—"The Sweetest Kill," a song that was written in 2010 but which I had never heard until last night, at a bar on Smith called Hunters. Go figure.

Everything comes back to death, desire, the poetry of the body and the body of poetry that lives in the folds of skin and sensation: this flicker between being and not being, if not being could also permit the conditions to turn flesh into a written word. To pursue each, to pursue both at the same time—a desire to die into feeling; is that what writing is, what it nurtures, what it destroys? Is that what it means to put my hand here and inscribe you too? Escrito sobre un cuerpo. Hunters. All of us.

♦

I calmly got undressed, hung my jeans over the back of a chair, and slid into bed, doing it the way I would if I were the one watching it happen. It felt good to be there, naked, and alone, and the pillow as soft as your skin, or mine, just not in winter, because that's when my body sometimes gets dry, and patchy, and prickly, like I'm burning to get out of it. Something I wish for a lot.

♦

& years ago
I worked for a spell
as a mannequin
without a shirt & wearing
jeans blue denim etched
an emblem meant
to represent some
small bird torn
below the hip
& at the knee
I couldn't say & neither was I
permitted to speak
so I'd often think
standing still, taut &
exhausted
with persons who wanted
to be in pictures, spell-
bound but also bounded
(another double-

decker rushes by, another
outburst of light)
how many others have lived
this dream
or died so I might
dream about it?

♦

The feeling of knowing everything was about to begin or had just begun, was forever always beginning or becoming. Becoming something else. And my future out on Atlantic waiting.

♦

I've been listening to the same song for days
watching heat & discharge shimmer off
the asphalt like tidal crush, distorting
or reforming everything, learning to
come on someone
else's command
is it enough
that we crave objects
that we are always looking
for a way out of objection
what's worse to know
the flesh disappears our bodies
& what's inside
dies or that we
believe it

♦

No one recognizes me unless you're there.

You told me, when I'd asked you if anyone recognized you at Brooklyn Roasting because we'd always gone there, because we went there just yesterday, which was the last time you went there, before today.

Was it so strange, I thought, to depend on another to be recognized for one's self. What do I have to do with your face, I asked, your lips and head, the cheek I've felt on my cheek so often, when I can't fall asleep? You didn't have an answer, then or now, when I posed a similar question. And the thing that was on my mind anyway was something you had no knowledge of, something I'd never told you, a game I used to play as a kid, maybe not a kid but a teenager, an adolescent as they say, sociologically speaking, eleven or twelve so maybe not teen, maybe just preteen, *pre*, that's the word, though I always hate saying it, even in my thoughts because it reminds me of the fact of my birth, or how much I must have missed in my mother's womb, forgetting for a moment what a head start I got on the living—the real thing and the rarest, right?—and anyway, the game was something you could play alone so it was ideal, for a certain child at a certain time, but even so, you had to play it in the company of others, people who were like actors without scripts, moving from the stage to the sidewalk and back again, and all I had to do was watch them pass but the thing is, no one could notice me watching or the game was up, the play was over, so I'd stay there, silent, watching, looking at one subject, a term I also find discomforting (why not just say "person"?) but which seemed appropriate given the context, except

I didn't think of it like that, not like *subject* and not like *context*, not at twelve and definitely not at eleven, one classmate at a time, one chaperone, one teacher, picking up on their mannerisms and how they changed, if they changed at all (they always did) when they saw someone else or when they saw someone was watching, someone else besides me, I mean, and how things would shift—a wrinkle near the eyes, a smirk, a bend in the elbow, the caress of one hand as it is held by the hip—or how they would, in spite of one's awareness of being watched, stay the same, and what that meant, which was the most important thing to me, the motivation or logic behind it, if it was measurable, if I could pinpoint it or make it stick, and then repeat it, make it repeat, these people and their performances and me in my seat in the front row, which was the best seat in the house, and the only one.

♦

I don't know what else to say. I could say I knew this was coming. (How could I not know this was coming?) Now I'm yours to hold and keep, or to swallow and shit out. I'd do the same thing, if I were in your place. If I were you. My hunger is hungrier than the stars.

the big ship [musical interlude]

0:01

In the afternoons, my eyelids stir like woods. Like sky and skin.

In the evenings. In the mornings.

0:17

So cold I start to cry. Or maybe just the force of the act. Recognition, waking. Waking and running and crying at the same time.

0:32

If I know the route well enough, I can close my eyes.

The deliberate buildup of percussion, mallets or castanets, any and all expectation. The way a snake moves through the brush.

Something that resembles rivulets, people and places and things swiftly pushing forward. Pulsing into feeling.

1:00

But I never forget to collect random samples.

numb cheeks
ashen sand

tracks left by an excavator
a leaf slowly falling through my gaze

1:33

Certain uncertain ideas about love. The nature of wanting and possession. Terminal inertia. Holes in the soles of my shoes.

How maybe the gap is intended. Cavity, lacuna. Depression around the short bend, something that provokes. How maybe it's better this way.

You're moving faster now.

2:08

Pause before the applause
You imagine at some other time
In another place

2:25

We keep passing, every day.

Silent smiles with each exhalation and raised foot, and then you're just a figure receding into dawn. Legs kicking in the distance.

2:47

Unbearable glare of the sun on my face, or the face I imagine as light ripples over the Hudson, breaking and receding like a fractured mirror.

Discarded Photoville stubs in between cracks of gravel. Faces degraded in gelatin for posterity, and a fee. A fence to frame it.

I can smell the coffee brewing. I can smell the people moving. Hair and breath and sweat and shit mingling in the breeze.

Some person is still dreaming.

3:03

Each and every time you try to write it down, memorize a sunrise for later (always for later). The sound and shape. Each thin gradient. Each slow unfurling.

3:05

Sometimes I just like to hear my own expiration.

Hint in story; or, slat of glass that became a face, that became a life. (Shift all instances of the past to the present when reciting this aloud, like a photo of a photo of a photograph in which we ask, without the mark that desires a response:

Where is the original event.

) The curve of interlude that begs separation and distance; that begs proximity, since every intermission is an excuse to return. When I am not writing I want to be writing and when I am writing I do not want to pause, not for anything, least of all hunger.

(I write to glut myself on words.)

When I stall long enough to look up (while reading), I can remember what I liked most about movies: the holes in the film, out of which stories other stories emerged. What I wish for (even now, in memory's altered gaze) is to produce discrepancies, like the delay in the dub, or the black spots on the cellulose that remind me I am rubbing my eyes as I retrieve this scene among any others. How I can forget everything about her except for her voice, or the way his mouth refuses to move when I write out a list of ten questions I'd had in my head and which remained there, images stuck on a spool when the projector jams; like the lag between lips and when sound moves in—enough time to adorn the story in omission, to write (recite, paint, or otherwise record) by cutting (details, didn't you know? were meant to be cut). I heard the tale is the most common form of inheritance, a narrative belonging to no one, belonging nowhere, exceeding the territorial and the individual, propelled across borders on the condition only that it keeps passing.

I heard that lyric began in the absence of sound, or the absence of its reception; music that passes unheard. I meant to write: music that passes *because it remains unheard.*

What scared me as a child was not silence but speech. So unsure of how a word will sound when it falls from my mouth. I don't want to tell you about myself but some of these ingredients, I wonder, are necessary.

Te voy a enviar. He writes, I'm going to send you. Maybe he meant send for you. Maybe there is a word missing (there is always a word missing). Maybe he meant, I'm going to send you, as in move or bring you, as in I am still here, waiting to be transported, like clandestine information, or illicit goods. Find another word for *contraband*. If this I were me, instead of my father, I would think about all the many ways to picture rendition, and all the many cities in which his son (another I) could have been born besides this one, where we've met in the space of a text, which is still occurring. Video, from the Latin *videre*: to see. Video cassette recorder, first use: So that the television does not have to be adapted to take the recorder, the VCR is put between the TV and its aerial. I, too, need your help for this, I often think. Because even the moving image (projected up there, so high) relies on the effects of the audience members, who mimic the camera. Convergence of the body of the film and the body on film, and also, as you know, the bodies outside the film: subjects and objects and spirits of the air linked through likeness and substitution. The whirl made flesh.

If the tracking is off, it is because the magnetic media within each tape has degraded: a loss of lubricant in the binder, since successive recordings strip a layer of information each time we record something new. If the tracking is off, it is because the path of exile is susceptible to degeneration. What is unrepresentable—remember—is not the same as what is an alternative to representation.

Whenever I picture their faces, I picture each one half-formed; I wait for expression, for the pinch or wrinkle in the cheek, between the eyebrows (contraction of the grief muscle). A wave breaking in reverse. A cloud doodling the sky.

playback

the outsiders

He often spoke about the life of the mind, and not just the life of the mind but its history, an internal history that could only be experienced and that, despite or maybe exactly because of its inability to be recorded for later, indicated our culture's solitary resistance to the history of the public, the past we have inherited and the past we accept, perhaps out of fear for an unceremonious annihilation.

Sometimes I prefer to think that the book he's making—compiling the text as if it were a heap of misplaced objects, using the page as a mantel for their unsettled reunion—the book is not about the migratory routes of his mother and father, or what it was they found when they each arrived, besides a life, besides a place in which to live, but his own ability to feel out of place wherever, wherever he found himself.

The leaves were just beginning to turn, from emerald to a bright fiery red, and the variations of orange into yellow, and there was a light breeze coming in from the East River that cooled my bare legs as we sat, under the shade of a tented roof, and I listened while taking notes, should I ever find a use for the descriptions of the lecture hall, or what it was they spoke about, if they spoke at all during a seminar that she'd visited as a guest, sitting at the far back of the airy auditorium as he spoke to his students about the fetishization of the original, and our tendency to ascribe it with an assumed authenticity, or whether it isn't true that there was a mode of expression, that there were a great many texts that, in actuality, were born in translation, since some things come secondhand if they come at all, urging his students, she said, to reevaluate the gravity we so often place on firsts, whereas I also remember, he acknowledged on that day, that things are greater—aren't they?—whenever we insisted it would be the last time. As I said, if I should ever find a use for any of this, except I knew that the only reason I was able to continue paying my rent for so long, with my head above water as they say, was to find a use for everything. Unless it was to be good for nothing.

I said "ability," she cut in, sometime later, and by then we were already onto other subjects: another swift uptick in antisemitism, a Philadelphia man who ate a rotisserie chicken every day for nearly six weeks, midterm elections, the price of eggs. But what I meant was "curse."

footloose

If I told you it was boredom would you believe me? If I told you and you heard me, if I told you and you listened. Could you hear it? And would we put it to music? Would we dance? If we weren't so bored and would we like it.

Boredom has a peculiar sound, a sound like a vacuum, one of those portable vacuums that runs on batteries and fits in the nook of your arms, to be cradled and carried to another room, and another room, and another room ... or the sound a refrigerator makes when you swing it open, thrust your face in. Swoosh. Sometimes when I'm so bored I try to swallow it down, the way I can swallow almost anything. Swoosh.

I consider all things and all lines and all persons and the moments shared between us as titles waiting to happen.

Permission slip.
Hard, to tell.
Young skin runs.

People tell me all the time young skin must run in the family. The family to which they refer, the family they've never met, is mine. I wonder what's the difference between young skin running and old skin running, and the destination of the jog or sprint if it's not death; if it's not death that we are constantly running toward, always and at the same time toward both growth and decay, like flexing, like a muscle being flexed, which means I'm being torn, which means I'm being reshaped, loudened, enlarged. A thing cuts so it can be fleshed out. I'm talking about books again, I'm talking about the people holding them: each a willing patient on the operating table.

But I'd like to linger on the flesh, the cut, the groove, the edge, the nick and friction of a word when it's still in your mouth. The scratch that is both redaction and accumulation, remix and master track. Absent ink or a computer, I would write this letter out from scratch.

I want to tell you this fascination with running is a fascination for form—to imagine a body always in motion means to imagine a body that can't be fixed. You have my permission to slip, and in slipping, to slip yourself in a little deeper, to the point that measurements can no longer be rendered; they must be imagined. As if you could just turn back the time that had already passed, that was already passing, cancel out experiences, as if you could revert or reverse, as if you could re: verse. Sometimes I think this shared correspondence is an exchange of anonymous encounters, because I'm not sure who I am when I write to you; I'm not sure who's inside of me and when. And then what? When the subject becomes reversible with the sender, the receiver becomes subject to rupture, too. I want to know what *that* sounds like. Pop. Or maybe another swoosh. Like the fizz that is still swirling on my tongue in a Kodachrome photograph of me as I turned ten. At some point I was nine. Just before if not after. As if you could just decide what should be forgotten and what should be remembered. I always think, *This is what you came for.* And I mean it.

The way all the photos we decide to share today are missing the negatives.

Anyone who ever took "out of sight, out of mind" at its word doesn't understand the seduction of appearances. To be in front of you, then, to be above you, to be below me. Anyone who's ever written a letter understands this desire of distancing, of the distance I would like to create only so I can be filled by it, only so I can be flushed out and have to fill the space again: your body, your fingers on the pulse of the key (I can hear the gesture a letter makes when the flesh approaches, the index and the middle digits, and even more, the faint exhalation a moment after the flesh departs). I would like you to only ever be out of sight so that I could place you in my mind, so that I could see you again, and see you differently.

What is a letter but the desire to be torn by you? To be turned by you to turn into you? And the condition to pay in advance.

And I do it like a dog. And I do it with my eyes closed. And I do it with my legs crossed and the humming machine hovering above my hips. Really.

(A vision of Derrida tearing up all his letters and throwing them in the Seine, as crowds of pedestrians and policemen watch. A vision of Derrida saving up all the money he makes on the lecture circuit in '77 to purchase an answering machine. What the sand remembers to forget.)

I imagine the scene of your reception the way I imagine my own funeral. Music plays idly, people come and go, your legs dangle and gyrate from a seat or stool, a pumpkin pie lies untouched, in its ovoid plastic home, preserved for all time. *Vitrine*. What a word.

I imagine the time difference between us the way I imagine a plate of pancakes on my bed, and I am eating through you to the other side. Believe me.

It's hard to tell. And the thing to remember in the telling is that exposure takes time. I'd like you to develop these negatives six years from now. Show me how

We come out.

license to drive [suburban dust]

laboring on my job
search profile I
finally decide upon people
pay me to teach them how to forget

whatever they've been taught
about writing poetry   body?
I think or ante
body? I only wish to expire

Like the MetroCard I am holding in my hand as I type this, as I swipe and swipe and swipe again, no repetition without deliverance and no deliverance without repetition, which is about doing nothing, or going nowhere, or unsuccessful transmission. To complete all of these without completing anything is to flow or seep, to advance by retreating, at least to the MTA machine to press my flesh into the black and come back. Differently.

Suburbia accumulates dust the way trees accumulate names.

If I wasn't here, I'd be tanning in my parents' backyard, where the neighbors can watch from their rolling lawns or high windows. Surveillance, etymologically, always comes from above. I want to allow for another kind of valence or veil-ance or vigilance, one that comes from within, and one that comes from without. I am talking about my general absence, my disavowal of clothes, my supple body, which is both wanting and self-assured in the sun, on the granite tile, in the shadow of a tree that is preparing a lunch for our imagination, below my neighbor's gaze. Haven't dreams always liked to perch on high?

V thought the experience of modernity was acceleration. Another way of saying this is we were all getting closer to God. I mean death. I mean this Dairy Queen drive-thru where braking isn't even necessary. I open my mouth and say ahhh in merry-go-round stupor. Orgies were made for desultory window shopping, or game show mania played on repeat. I close my eyes so I can better taste victory. I close my eyes because everything else is open.

I like to imagine the Spanish version of this text. I like to imagine the German and the French. And here I am thinking about the person translating. And here I am thinking about the person who is ferrying me across the threshold of language, toward phatic communion or, better still, silence.

ghost in the machine

And he remembered the jazz singer and especially the jazz singer's voice during an interview he watched on one of the many numberless nights of insomnia that had afflicted him throughout his twenties, the way the woman laughed when she was asked if she'd ever had stage fright during her long and storied career, in which she played to sold-out clubs and lounges and evening galas and back-alley artist salons across France, and Spain, and in the autonomous regions separating the Swiss Alps from the Eastern Alps of Australia and the Italian after she'd toured all along the United States—it wasn't stage fright, but rather the common fright of the phonograph that seemed often to shake me into silence, so afraid was I to make a false note on the record, and for the mistake to be reproduced and circulated, and it was a kind of quaint phenomenon, I'll say, even though by now—my goodness, years later—we take it for granted, how the audiences would clamor for the studio version up on the vaudeville stage, how the recording had started to replace the live performance, not just as a preference but a form of expectation, since what technology wants, he thought then, while he was enduring another long and sleepless night, was to remove traces of the human in the art, and even as she, on screen, continued talking to a man he couldn't see, a man that was never shown—only a voice, as if inserted in post—he'd stopped listening for the sake of continuing his own line of thought, thinking how often the role of technological mediation was to forget the fact that there ever was a human behind the machine. The days and nights continued like this, as if tuning a radio or flipping the channels; in that amorphous way dreams have of producing space as an amorphous zone, so, too, was this decade of insomnia responsible for the slippage of such found footage into the details of his own transient life, as one applies color to the image, or reverb to the master track, retrospective attempts to create depth, texture, and the impression of cohesion.

On other days (other nights), he preferred to explore the flight of discharge and emergence without committing it to writing, perhaps under the pretext, veiled as a question: Does an image destroy the imagination? Memory, too, was another kind of translation, and just as unfaithful, just as true.

tremors

Source the etymology of nickname. Where does sensation go if and when it leaves the body. The erratic ride of muscle. Tendency to lift my head (to the sky). Tendency to rift meanings behind certain words for a subscription. Because neither of us knows how, we will learn together. Think of something you did once, I'll say, which begs to be slow-motion lathered. Want these words, too, to serve as spell, the quiet oblivion of watching (to crush and be crushed, to be so swiftly undone). Shock of arrival when I rest my thigh here. Dedicated my life to the immediacy of wonder.

l'avventura

If there's a train, there's a man running after it.

♦

We agree to meet at a bar.

He walks in from the dusk, sunspots lingering on his cheeks. As if lit from within. The camera pans across the room to show the eyes, how each face turns.

I'm pretending to be on the phone.

Something to hold.

♦

The scene involves climbing a fire escape with a bouquet of roses, conquering a fear of heights with music and a kiss.

♦

The illusion of being in someone else's possession.

♦

He'd run by her home every morning.

He didn't know if he was more afraid of seeing her, or not seeing her. Every morning.

♦

As the two lovers talk, the Amalfi coast rushes by, slow enough to catch a glimpse, quick enough to want to catch it in place. The camera focuses on their faces, each exchange cropped in medium shot, leaving the site secondary, letting the setting recede into a fabulous black-and-white blur.

♦

I kept looking for suggestions of his presence, as if he were everywhere. As if he's everywhere. The bend at a corner. Silhouette turned toward a streetlamp. Puddles on the sidewalk. Especially, behind the window. Tracks left by sandals on the prefab beach, sand driven in from somewhere else. On a day like this.

♦

Hoist a boom box over your shoulder, a friend says, and blast the song to which you both first fell in love on a loop.

♦

The soft blush of flowers. Lonesome whistles. Press my ear to a tree and listen.

♦

How, she wondered, am I supposed to know whether two people can fall in love at the same the very same time?

♦

The airport, right before takeoff. Someone is always arriving, or leaving. Or taking. Or off.

Pull back from a piece of luggage, the roving escalator in the distance. Shouts and the skid of rubber, loud enough to turn around.

The camera encircles them in wild swoops. Reverse angles. It makes you lightheaded, just to watch it happen, just to see it outside yourself.

♦

The way she points her thumb and index finger to salvage the crumbs.

♦

The reason or one reason why song is so beautiful is that it is temporal. Three minutes, four. Epiphany with a countdown.

♦

Such a long take between when our eyes finally meet—me still clutching my phone, speaking to no one—and when she glides forward, drifting as if being carried. Glass chandelier, a bar with shelves that reach toward the ceiling. A fireplace and exposed brick. Soft shadows. Entrance of a piano without anyone seated to play. Kind of place with a coat check girl and a man that opens doors. In the bathroom, for the privilege of watching me empty my bladder, he asks for money, preferably bills.

Green with envy; wanting to be outside at the same time I'm within it. Wanting to remember the first time as if it were still the first time.

As if it were five minutes later, when we'd looked at each other from across the room and it started to come down.

♦

There's a French saying. Or at least I heard it said in France. There is one who is loved, and one who does the loving. And what then, when one becomes the other?

This would come right after the opening credits but before the names dissolve into a panorama of Brooklyn Bridge Park.

♦

Best to meet a man who's already moving. Capable of flight or fancy.

All the strangers who would not be strangers disembark, moving through Grand Central like a billiard ball, slipping in between each other on a dolly, crosscut with a close-up of the station's clock, the big and little hands.

Through a bus's cloudy window, the city looks unexpected, caramelized and soaked in sepia, strange landmarks spinning toward the audience like a carousel with every twist.

♦

Hunger for everything I've never had, for everything I've ever had.

Wondering what it was Meat Loaf wouldn't do after all.

♦

Tell me more.

♦

Aerial shot of the bridge during a storm, gaze slowly edging toward the promenade. A city that could be your own. Two figures at a stoplight. Lightning that sounds more like laughter than shrieks. Slow dancing as a form of silence.

♦

I put you into my memories for a purpose.

♦

Something has been left out, but I don't know what. A wipe, change of scene, sound of rainfall to match each pearl of rain, the passage of time.

I don't know what. Only enough to know something has been left out. Only enough to know something is missing. The way you sit with your palms touching and wait for it. Even after the lights go.

Even after everyone else has left.

la piel que habito

Tell me when you close your eyes where is it you go what is it you like to see how large is the picture when you enter and how does the sun feel the smell of a story when it's being told I mean being heard I mean recorded. He starts there then asks why my back is arched this way why my torso unfurls like a ribbon when you move your head like so and in such a turn. I want to show you the rhythm of my speech when I am only thinking. I want to show you I know what it is and how to die.

v is for vendetta

In my favorite anaerobic class on a Wednesday morning, I am the only one wearing mesh shorts, so loose that when I perform a single jumping jack my unsheathed orbs, both and with different patterns of aplomb, extend themselves in the cool clarity of viridescent studio lighting and the fractions of sunlight persisting between plastic slats of window.

I like a breathless 16:9 widescreen format, the smell of uncut grass and how the density of the air shifts, just by leaping in place, with my legs kicked out and my arms unfurled like a map of Blue Beard's lost treasures.

Picture me with bare shoulders and a lily tucked behind an ear, listening to that good music that permits a certain confidence and makes you feel powerful, where power is really a construction of feeling, and feeling a substitution for touch. What I am speaking about is the desire to pass the world through a body and to have that body record the variations of throb and boredom, boredom and throb.

Among my aspirations is equal opportunity for pleasure upon all bodies, regardless of shape, size, and genre. Why can't I, too, be shucked like a happy hour oyster emblazoned with sea salt and a generous squeeze of citrus, the companionship of a roommate's shower sponge when it feels like a milk bath in your cheeks or the first time you used a bidet.

So then what happens when you look up a word you don't know to find another word with which you are also entirely unfamiliar? Oblanceolate means inversely lanceolate, as in an oblanceolate leaf. A leaf which is not at all visible in my camera eye because of issues with learning, or my particular upbringing. Specific to a deficiency in botanical education, or a broken English I don't feel like mending.

Never have I ever seen the sprawling city streets from the top of a red double-decker omnibus, nor have I been the microphone placed in your furious grip as I lean over and ask whether this thing is on, and if it is: *would you like me to go louder?*

A story might start like this. In another room like and unlike this one, on the sixteenth floor of a building between avenues eight and nine, a photoshoot is occurring. Light claps through the cloudless afternoon at a clip of 7.8 seconds. So quick, it's possible, I guess, to mistake each shot with a shriek of lightning, or a chorus of angels (a chorus of sighs). To test the tightness of the skin we stretch it vertically and bounce a quarter against my upper thighs.

One of my most rapturous pastimes is pouring seltzer water into a glass and waiting to hear the crystalline liquid gurgling back a possible response to my inquiry concerning IKEA's Swedish meat-balls, or the perfumed charcuterie awaiting me back home, thin ribbons of factory handled Genoa salami, which reminds me of desires to be torn, like the uncharacteristically deep V neck with which I absconded from the dressing room of an Urban Outfitters

that is no longer & nowhere
have I found such brazen sun

tanned confidence as the small
space for withdrawal bisecting
the sales floor with cut
rate drapes, an urban outfitters
that is now a petco unleashed

where my scapula &
tease of sternum
furnished by an unfinished
cleave or the negative
space probed by deep
V's commitment
to depth decoy
my inability to exist without
theft in the middle of the day

when what was stolen was a glance when a glance
meant the satisfaction of anointing aloe vera below
my clavicle, the hardest parts
which are the most vulnerable
the numberless tourists, who name
these gleaming rivulets of sweat
& their resistance to collar suffocation

So I fear these things within myself when I begin to recognize them in others. When I am at my most vulnerable, for instance, I escape toward the perspective of my low-waist satin thong, relishing the cracked vibration between garment and flesh, the punctum of every image which is also its wound, but all I have today is the indecisiveness of baggy mesh shorts at my favorite donation-based high intensity interval training for young professionals, each mistimed jumping jack evidence of my ritual displacement into memory: Genoa salami, Urban Outfitters, mineral oil applied unsparingly, Unleashed, which, unlike its Petco parent store, does not sell live animals, shower sponges and public bidets, the deep V I haven't paid for, this photo shoot on the sixteenth floor, which is still occurring—irresistible rust of experience reduced to a high-resolution image burned on your screen. Haven't you ever wanted to look up the definition of *girder*?

A horizontal main structural member that supports vertical loads and that consists of a single piece or of more than one piece bound together. But the detail to which my eye keeps returning is *vertical loads*. The admiration and the hospitality; the terror and the awe. I have never heard the word before, nor have I ever seen a girder in "real life." Nevertheless, let the V in V neck stand for *vertical*; let our consensual desire to pursue the support of indiscriminate and manifold vertical loads overwhelm this voice memo, since the first cut, I've heard, is the deepest. Deep V consciousness: the coy interjection of lubricated flesh amid the raunch of daybreak, unashamed and unreasonably unresistant, like a souffle corsage and the luminous exhale, and how I long to be both had and taken; to be scandalized by a deep V whose intensified nadir edges toward the striations of buttered muscle that signal the arrival of my pecs. If I am my V neck, instead of the body wearing it, I am both a vertical load and the horizontal main structural member that supports it. If writing really is a slow, slippery striptease, may this voice-over transcription serve as the viewer's own undeniable deep V, whose name in my search field reveals that users also ask: "Why do I look better in V necks?" In a choose your own adventure novella, I was never asked to decide between crew necks and V necks, or maybe I refused to honor the proposition. It reminds me that so very often the choice is already made for us. And then what? The repetitive circular motion of your hand, or rumor of America: the bloated promise of a country in which one can arrive in an ordinary crew neck and walk out with several varieties of deep Vs in assorted colors and fabrics, even if you've never paid. It's a dream, really, the hallucination of endless inventory, the freedom to keep spending. This is why my parents came. The joy of repetition, a jutting neckline that bulges with hope and manic hunger. See Jack Jump, the jumping jack, also known as a side-straddle hop, or a star jump. I keep returning to an original position, despite or maybe because of my desire to move beyond myself, to look back, to return your glance with my outstretched arms, the outline of unveiled latency resembling a V.

the lost boys [suburban lust]

In pursuit of Suburban Lust I return, from time to time, to the town of my adolescence, ghosting the pale gray corridors of a high school and its strobe-lit spring socials whenever I stop to think or refrain from thought, for once and all at once. A man I've never seen before solicits my neck to say: I have a ripped T-shirt with your face on it.

I want to know where the rip is, but I don't ask. I only look for it in the mirror of others, chalk up the episode to the total gift of forgetting or of being forgotten, the hypnotic notion of being out of print in the era of post internet. *As Humpty Dumpty says about some of his more remarkable words, "I pay them extra, and make them do what I want."*

This inscription or annotation or meditation, like many others, deserves a discovery of relation among events that appear to coexist "at random." Classic case: a member of the audience wants to know if my new book is unreadable. The need to recover from certain books, films, TV shows, art installations interests me. I am interested in alternating currents of drainage and recovery, the recovery of the reader-viewer, who has lost their mind. And gained something else, which I do not wish to describe here. The member of the audience turns around and walks away, without saying good-bye. In general, I expect to be overstimulated. I am preparing, I say to no one but myself, for my own overstimulation. Feed on the rare fruit—

the second piece
of advice
I offer on first dates

since everything round invites
a caress, since every caress
invites the friction where

imagination meets memory
the voluptuousness of high or hard-to-
reach places, the other side of zero

(A VR simulation set in 2056 from the perspective of people playing it in 2097)

In a dream, or memory, I'm flirting with several different lift boys, riding the elevator all the way to the top of the Empire State Building and back to the lobby, which resembles the Beverly Wilshire, in *Pretty Woman*. Aleatoric caresses in the backseat of a taxi speeding through Midtown, which is always the site of a speeding taxi when no one is watching it pass. To tell the truth, it's hard to tell, given my delusion of doubles for which everything is familiar and nothing is recognizable.

And so I fantasize about swift encounters in shopping malls, forget-me-nots under a marquee or the pause before boarding another roving staircase, the deft drift toward ecstatic consumption where invitations linger to shop till we drop, desiring nothing except the taut moments of torment or betrayal that offered itself up on rainy days, or weekends, or whenever I was thick with panic;

the horror of being stuck in my own skin. I fantasize about a region beyond memory, recalling that nothing is ever empty or full for those dreamers who dream of holes.

Aspiration: to write a book that can be interrupted at any moment w/o losing its momentum. Escape dodge and deviate from any and all criteria of "success" ...

Aspiration: to catalog a series of firsts before they happen.

some days I think of myself
as meat or cream or a certain kind

of fruit which turns
without moving anywhere at all

I want to make myself available
to a nondescript "shock"

knowing what will happen to me and how
soon I say yes to everything asked

of me and the things which no one
has wagered to ask   actors

aren't any use for the five-minute
film I want to produce

a voice modeled on the voices
of others   I only want to come out or come out

of order   the conquest of hardness
can carry so far   the self

that learns from the performance   and God too
saw that it was good

I tell students my practice is to write on the subway or the bus, in the spare moments between floors or the opening of doors, against the window of a cruising jet, in the pause of light shifting. May I suggest we only ever discover ourselves when we're moving. A self-awareness through ejection or ejaculation, indiscrete or indiscreet moments when a knob wants to turn. And if you were still watching I'd beg critical detachment mixed with recreational jouissance.

Elsewhere, I am attentive to bone loss. How much bone have I lost since the moment I began writing this? In pursuit of Suburban Dust I return to the town of my adolescence, time to time to time to time, one word away from my favorite Cyndi Lauper, swaying nondescript trees and the smell of chemically-torn grass, my chemically-torn flesh susurrating underwater in the deep end before I come up for air. A thousand diving-board creaks as we hold for applause. The sound of news coming in. The sound of *new* coming in, which never actually arrives—this being the major selling point of suburban New Jersey, despite its praenomen: a propensity to satiate stillness, to cultivate a space where nothing ever happens—a rendering of stupor that allows me to merely drip my consciousness into yours, or to shamefully let myself leak out. Even so, resistance can be pleasurable and we should search for it, we should labor toward it, we should start by rubbing up against one another until we rub ourselves out. The way orchids thrive on moisture. The shudder of colors. And then the punctum from *The Lost Boys*: the poster of a shirtless Rob Lowe hanging in Corey Haim's bedroom. I want to say the difference between rapture and rupture is only one vowel. I want to say keep touching it, please. Which is always my advice to writers and editors and other readers interested in entering my text. We might as well call it the lyric essay. We might as well call it improvisational jazz. I know I've done my job if I can see my carcass on the floor, naked, breathless, but no longer self-assured. I know I've done my job if we can mark my unraveling. If we can measure the duration of flight. If we can see with another's eyes, speak from another's throat. If we can savor the lacteal mouthfeel, the gauzy suction burst of unbecoming. I heard diving is disastrous for the soul.

interview with the vampire

A day just like any other, I caught myself becoming what I am no longer, shedding accents gradually, re-forming a face, surprised by my own sweat, surprised by the fact of my replica, or what has been replaced (wet lips, tepid expression). I dreamed a dog was digging me out.

He could feel the moment moving.
He could feel it rotating.

They were pulling my leg or at least pushing it into place when a tear appeared. I searched myself for a line or lines, remembering at the apex of my veer what the diagram looked like before I'd retraced it.

So many attempts to recall the smell of time, the sea in evening, a tourniquet of words to stop his mind from bleeding out, to stop the image from receding (amnesia sadness, or aphasia). Vista of a single vanishing point where even wind has a name, where even he recognizes himself in photographs; the eyes that stare, and stare back.

Arrange my solitude, cauterize and clothe me, bisect me in squares (as big as a box, eight by ten with a price tag affixed in front), dispose me in a holiday greeting, stamped and packaged, picked apart at customs for being deemed dangerous. Beauty is always arresting. I come just by listening.

28 days later

Delayed again like I never left, hardly touching ground—took a detour in Rome[6] (these things I learned in school); people can be so cruel, tour guides whispering in Italian—stupid Americans standings hands on hips with their fanny packs strapped around their waist; I pretended not to know; I pretended not to notice. I stopped in Paris, paid to piss. I'd been walking for miles; I'd been spent. Tired, penniless. I bathed in the bathroom of Charles de Gaulle, stuck my head under the faucet, ran the water over everything that would fit. He was smiling like a skeleton when he telephoned. Once held a skull with his bare hands, he said, stuck his fingers through the opening where the eyes had been (out of sight, out of mind). He said death was trending. He said an explosion to the face revealed character. He said a lot of things, that guy, the other guy. Everything starts to look the same the more you look at it—indecipherable, black spots on the film, any point on a map, a button pressed on the camera slung around my

---

[6] I never knew

in which direction

to go: up, up

down, down

left, right, left

three-hundred-twenty steps

up the basilica

all the way

so many lives await

neck. Take your pick. I'm just a tourist. I just came for the pictures. Casualties in a market, casually walking through; pardon me, this must be the place. In Cannes, the sky was purple and the moon was red. In London, I walked over so many dead.

la notte

I could press myself against this foam roller, similar to how your body is expanding across the hood of a car, in a music video I can't look away from. I could record the sound of my writing voice, and I could play it back into the room again and again and again. As we think about foaming the soft tissues of our "problem areas" each in our separate space, with the camera settings set to blur, and the electric progressions of pop rock I've muted for our purposes, a song which you've been hired to dance to. Every recording becomes a reading, which is performed by the one listening. This is the part where you continue, or begin. What I mean or what I am trying to say is I am writing in a room I imagine to be your own. What you mean or what you are trying to say is again and again and again.

And again and also   sometime later:

(This is the pretty part of the poem or the part of the poem that pretends it is something other than what it is, or what it will be. To make this part we've already switched places; I am asking, now, to be the room you are sitting in. To do this I need to open wide, or wide enough to have you climb inside me.)

♦

On line or in line (between two points or places in a general line or one as specific as the checkout), I wait for a question: to be asked to speak, to rush the air out, to move my right hand from my left hip, to reach, to retch yet quietly, to wet my lips, to bite down or clench, to lean or bend, to turn my wrist, to open my palm, to shift my gaze, to slip or slide into, to ask for to be asked after, to appear as something other than a ghost.

the passenger

How often naked, or picturing yourself nude, all the people looking like the walking dead stumbling from their Brooklyn Heights homes, slipping in and out like a vestibule or a sweater vest, heads down, giving signs of a cross (between languid and impatient), sending messages so long they never reach intended recipients, dearly departed or sent back with such hush and expectation; talking with someone who is someone else while we while away the hours, as they say or said so many years ago (a dreamy fascination on the nightstand). The one nightstand I own is well-worn and splintered at the edges, passé as an American journalist's hairline. Such a human desire to escape one's self back to Italian cinema, yellows and reds, the color of involvement.

(you're getting warm)

The last passage shows a school car pulling away in the twilight; the camera holds on a hotel as the credits begin to roll. To say you got it is to say no longer or never again; filigreed my existence for a royalty you can find among the stacks, if you're persistent. So what's your deal? they keep asking, as if this were a business, as if this were an indefinite quantity of moving images: a stranger's high five seen from misted windows, lit up cheeks, nondescript sirens, a tongue around a ring pop (as seen from the tendered hand). We call the time between the end of the final visible line of a frame and the beginning of the first visible line of the next frame a *vertical blank interval*.

There's something beautiful about an ass in slow-motion, how you always remember it afterward or elsewhere like sitting on a twin bed with the one you adore and having u can't touch this come on the radio, MC Hammer and my my my my thoughts colliding to form another song

still singing when the shower stops (a bridge over troubled puddles) and when you're asked to dance you leave footnotes all over the floor, moaning like David as he continued to pose; you can't fake a thing like that and how. Always and from an early age so gaga over chiasmus, exchange, discrepancy, questions of tempo and mood.

(you're getting warmer)

When the boat capsized and the men all drowned in the porous space between continents (between nations, between states), they returned each night, in the bodies of the lovers they'd left behind. If I could return as anything other than what I was, I'd choose the damp blouse worn by the ex-journalist who wrapped it against his palms before he buried the stranger he resembled and whom he felt he would become.

cold war

I gathered myself in the mirror. I gathered myself from what was left behind, which is another word for future. All the many mouths of trees, the eyes of bushes I've wanted to crawl inside. Use cherry as a verb. Learn and learn and learn again how to say all the French I've stirred into the pot in the voices I know by heart. All the French and the German too. The German and the French.

The past of dreams, dreams of the past.

My grandfather, the voice-over begins, passed away months before I was born. Holding his camera, a Soviet Zorki C (a Leica II reproduction), makes me feel connected to him in some way. Dark green, with a leather case in which to sit, the camera is hugged by a harness that used to hang from the wearer's neck, but the leather has dried out and the harness has ripped. Every time I press the shutter, the camera puffs out a little cloud. Every time, I try to hold it there, the little cloud I call film vapor.

What parts do I leave out when I cover a portion of this page with my palm. What parts let out when I forget to think long enough to feel. To come back to the part of a fan blowing in a circular motion in an otherwise motionless studio apartment. To come back to the part where I can't decide which is which, the past or dreams. Ancient axiom: as life grows longer, I bow down for blur. To rub it in, as if a cloth, the lotion or the skin itself. People say you can't take anything with you. So what is this then, the way it begins, and always "without warning."

fatal attraction

When I was here last, four years ago, I didn't come in on a half-empty jet; I wasn't sitting across from two guards clad in Joint Task Force Empire Shield uniforms.[7] When I was here last, four years ago, the only photograph I kept wasn't one I'd taken myself. I was mid-flight, or somewhere between flight, not before and not after, the interval between crouching and a leap, a leap and the body's total immersion into another body. I like the photo because of its indeterminacy, the undecidability of skin, the rim of a riverbank or a pool's edge, petals that resemble confetti stars. I like the photo because it's the only image I've ever been given in which I remain unrecognizable, even to myself.

---

[7]Joint Task Force Empire Shield, which was activated in response to 9/11, costs New York thirty-three million dollars every two years to maintain. I look this up with my left hand as I raise my right hand, to lift my mask, to pull it down so it hangs below my chin.

great expectations (1946)

I started noticing Jason Innocent's declarations in the fall of 2016. Maybe it was earlier. Maybe it was summer. They were always written in black. They were always written in lowercase, without periods, without commas, without the need—or desire—to close the communication. *all my friends are in my head,* reads one, at the entrance to the A/C on Adams Street. *these thoughts are wrong,* reads another, in the opposite direction, at the intersection of the entrance to the Brooklyn Bridge. *not doing anything* on the bus stop near the revolving door's entrance to MetroTech. And underneath all of them, *jason innocent,* usually written above or below, *on* and *in,* name and surname, overlapping, as though Jason, or whoever was inscribing each aphorism, was not really inscribing anything at all. It was more like they were trying to erase themselves. It was more like they were trying to rub themselves out.

I don't know why I think of this now, but I think of it. And I think if this were a film—another film, a different film—it'd be the opening scene. A slow pan from a Steadicam, the panorama of the promenade at dawn: a nameless future at the far edge of the frame.

♦

All the strangers I dream about, the strangers in my dreams, are not strangers at all but real people. I notice this while bartending at the Phillips Auction House on Park Avenue and 57th Street, a place I avoid if I can help it, if it's not somehow helping me, surrounded as I am by so many others, so many others like and unlike me, forced to become somebody else in the pursuit of becoming more of myself.

Twice a month I wear black slacks and a black tie and a black, slim-fit collared shirt, sleeves which I roll up, just below my elbows, to hand out champagne and a white wine, a Grüner or a Riesling, to several guests. The guests stay the same, the gallery changes. A black and white photo of Muhammad Ali standing over a face-less fighter mutates, weeks later, into a cubist rendition of Mickey Mouse. A World War II airfield shifts to the topography of Gisele Bündchen. But the guests don't morph, they just accumulate; they keep filing in. Asking for the same complimentary champagne, the same chilled Grüner or Riesling; they even ask the same questions, practicing different intonations. Is this a *dry* Riesling? Is that a *different* bottle than the one you'd poured *earlier*? The bubbles taste *different* … or: The *bubbles* taste different. And no one expects a response, not really. They only expect you to look them in the eye. Like you did four weeks ago, a month ago, three months ago, a year … The same people are cast in slightly different roles; they wear slightly different clothes; I recognize them, the way I recognize myself in old photographs. In a book I'm reading, someone is quoting someone else about the act of sublimation. "It is the ability to sublimate that makes an artist," the page I'm on, right now (so as to check), reads.

If this were a movie, the photo I'm standing behind would be before you. You'd be standing before the photo.

Several renderings of rectangles. Rectangles that resemble a microwave oven, an office desk, a television set from 1974. Three rows, three columns. All outlined in red.

Earlier, when thinking of this line and deeply afraid I would lose it, I nearly popped a guest's eye out uncorking a bottle of Prosecco. Champagne, right? the guest asks me, just now, as I find my phone to type this (I am still looking at him in the eyes). Yes, I reply, nodding with aplomb, even though the bottle is from a region of Italy I can't pronounce.

If I snuck this under you, do you think it would fit?

I lift my head to see another phone—not mine—and its white charger, the flesh that bears it, the flesh that offers it to me, that pleads for restoration. A question that is not a question but a command, since I'm already holding the phone, since I'm already plugging it into the outlet against my hip.

Before smartphones, people used to hold up mirrors in public to see what they were: a view of themselves outside of themselves. Nothing really has changed, when you think about it.

I am thinking about it. I almost say it out loud, and only because the view has shifted. I'm standing in front of something else now: a woman in a green floral dress standing behind a blue door, her right hand stretched behind her, as if she's pushing an invisible object or subject away, unless she's just creating space, making room for herself, the frame, the photographer. All of this presented in wide shot, exaggerated format of the cinema. In her right hand is a mirror, one of those small compacts people carry in their purses, except she doesn't have a purse. Her bobbed hair and floral prints and white-tipped nails suggest she's in the sixties, that this photo was taken in the sixties, maybe late fifties, maybe fifty-nine, unless all of this is just a re-creation. But, I thought then, like I'm thinking now, isn't everything a re-creation?

Anyway, the photograph. She's pale, she's brunette, she's beautiful in the way beauty is when we aren't thinking about it, and we can only see her right eye because her left is covered by the compact; she's covering her left eye with her left hand. It's almost like she's winking at us, unless she's winking at herself. After all, it's a mirror. The pleasure of seeing a new face, or the same face, which changes, minute by minute, every day. I haven't ever learned how to wink. If I weren't writing I'd be practicing in the mirror. I'd be really looking at you (in the eyes), which makes it harder but also more real. To learn to control my body in the presence of people.

Some strange scene. And all of this to tell you why.

But I keep doing it and doing it and doing it, like an infomercial, with that same kind of verve, too, with that same kind of vigor and bravura, a word I've never written before now. And desperation, too, at the same time and all the time; always with the same kind of desperation. Show off and show yourself, secretly hoping that the other person knows that you're performing and that they're performing too.

A person I dated for about a week, a week and a half, asks me, as we sit among froth and vapor in a high-end Japanese spa, if I am already using her as a character; if I am already using what I'd just told her, that whole thing about performing, about wanting the performance to come off well, but not too well, about wanting it to come off just enough so she could see it, sense in it her own performance, her own ability to be in solitude in the company of others.

I told her: This is getting too real.

We haven't spoken since. Now I wonder if what I wanted was the real thing after all. If what it is I ever want is the real thing and the rarest.

The problem with dating a writer is that inevitably, you become a part of the fiction. Subject, character, conflict. The fact that she'd already sensed this and was a willing conspirator had the opposite effect of collaboration. It terrified me. It was almost as if she became the mirror, as if she became the mirror instead of me. And now she was holding herself up so I could better see myself; so I could see myself for who I am, or everything I am not. It reminds me of something I heard just the other day, that the best place to hide a corpse is under everybody's eyes. And what have I been doing all this time but exhuming bodies?

When I was eleven, it occurred to me that it might be possible to have an interesting life (and all of this sounds so much better as I type this, because "When It's Cold I'd Like To Die" is playing, because the blinds are drawn, because I like the cold and I would never like to die, because it's 10:14 on a Saturday night and I'm not drunk, not even a little bit buzzed, not even a little bit torn from who I am at this very moment, seeing all things and everything simultaneously; maybe not seeing anything except what this is inside of me. In front of us.) I think I had just read a book, something aged, something passed down, secondhand. *Great Expectations*, probably. Something that shook me up; something that sent me somewhere outside myself. And it occurred to me that I might give that experience to someone else.

And "When It's Cold I'd Like To Die" shifts to "God Moving Over the Face of the Waters," and I sat here or I stood there, wondering about what this or that piece would fetch, wondering if I'd ever be asked my name—my real name—wondering when the party would end or if it had ever, really, begun.

When I was young, I didn't realize the effect of words, the effect of a single word. I didn't realize that every word and feeling was finding its own home within me.

When I was young, I never thought where I'd be, I never thought where life would take me, or how I'd make a living; how I'd make a life. When I was young, I only knew that I wanted to try as many things as I could, pick them up, try them on. I only knew I wanted to reimagine everything. I never got bored of that. I would never get bored of that. I was the child of two exiles after all, two people who learned to live by imagining the possibilities of *something else*. You could be anyone, I thought. Anyone, anyone.

♦

The letter I unfolded first was written in the same slender swooping characters to which I had grown accustomed, dotted with diacritics whose names I would have to, later, and when I emerged into daylight, look up: kreska, kropka, ogonek, and my favorite, the stroke, which pierces the *l* and turns it into an English *w*—abyss of the Polish alphabet, which I never learned to read but nevertheless admire with the curiosity and wonder of a hand-me-down Wnuk, my mother's surname, which means *grandson* in her mother tongue. The letter—a birthday greeting—was written to my mother but addressed to me, my seven-year-old self, on the occasion of turning eight, and I liked to follow the wobbly ribbons of blue ink with my finger, tracing the message as if copying out by hand was a method to imbibe the original, as if tracing my babcia's message twenty-five years later could return her to me and return us to ourselves, speaking without the need, or desire, to translate.

I return the letter to its withered envelope and place the flattened paper back in my messenger bag amidst the darkened faces that scuttle past, across the track aboard another train, careening on a different line, in the same or similar direction.

Another of my favorite pastimes is sending texts on subways without service. The idea of a message waiting for others. And all the messages waiting for me. The anticipation of it, the charge. Undercurrents of eroticism in every snaking train rattle, in every face seen through another train window, another train passing this one, and all the bodies you will never know, but in this glance.

The way I learn more about my body by watching yours.

♦

I like to go to museums and walk around and take photos of the people who are also walking around, some of them taking photos of the art, some of them taking photos of themselves, next to or in front of or surrounded by the work of so many others. Taking photos of people in an art museum is so much more interesting than taking photos of the art in an art museum because people's expressions change all the time, but the art seen today will look the same tomorrow. What's the point of another reproduction?

Which I guess you can say about a lot of things, probably too many to repeat here, and anyway, I'd already done too much of that earlier, before any of this, when I was just a face on a wall. Sometimes I still think of myself that way, held up without a frame, on a white wall like any other white wall: wan, waxy, ultra-white, a white wall that turns yellow if you stare long enough, if you're staring right now.

Details of characters emerge; my camera eye begins to cover their real faces, their real mouths and lips. The way one holds a flute, the way one guzzles down the liquid, how it clings against their teeth before the throat sucks it down, and with such a flourish; when they are looking at another guest and only pretending to listen, how their eyes betray their face, a disconnect that reminds me of desire. How it fixes in the gaze—always over the eyes and lips, over the expression in the cheeks, the chin—despite the pleasure being far below or deep inside, somewhere I shouldn't be able to see, not from my vantage, never, not ever.

♦

The last photo I remember, or the last photo I actually saw, before I left the gallery, the auction, all the guests I'd see again in four weeks, the same guests with slightly different names, slightly different ways of holding their hair, was a midnight blue watercolor interrupted with flashes of white letters, streaks of lightning graffiti against the night sky, which sketched: *It doesn't get any better than this.*

I remember shaking my head and smiling. I remember thinking: Of course it does. And that's why we're here.

man without a face

She has a square face with a strong jawline. Slight cheekbones, but they aren't prominent. My eyes are very wide set but also, she might have said, very deep set. They aren't quite any specific color, being mostly a dark grayish green with a circle of gold or blue around the pupil. She likes to think they are large, though they are often half closed in pictures. Probably, a viewer might think, because they have to hold the weight of her thick, long lashes. Lashes that repeat, that would be repeated, passed down, like almost anything. Visible and non-visible. So trauma leaks from a wound because some wounds never close. Despite this, some things cease in a single generation. The lips, for instance. Hers are slightly smaller than average; we were born in different countries, during different wars; she was, she would be my mother, despite our different mother tongues. Back to the face, the slight concavity of the bridge. The pale skin, so unpredictable in the summer.

I hear the camera's strobe and feel the warmth of the flashes on my face. The photographer's voice, the feeling of my own thoughts in my head and the sensation of my dry mouth. And then I remembered the single-propeller plane and the flags on the tarmac, drifting listlessly in the rising heat, flags which resembled the kites with which we'd race, if you could call it racing, on the roof deck; each terrace against every other, all of us children threatening to cut the rival kites at every turn; the cut-rate razors we'd wave, with performed menace, at the sky, which was not my own memory but my father's: the day dad departed a home to which he would never return, how he let his eyes trail off from the shimmering ribbons, following the different vehicles driving around the jet, how he traced its mechanical body, how he thought about the American film he saw just the other week, Marlon Brando dubbed into Cuban, which isn't the same as Spanish: the way everyone on screen convulsed, the way they danced, drunkenly, on the table before the music stopped; that a radio flung out the window was a way of speaking, for persons who could not name the unspeakable but nevertheless yielded to its design, as he looked at the cargo that continued to come out of the plane and wondered about each bag's contents, even though he knew the inside of every luggage was more or less the same: enough underwear, bras, and socks for a week, plus five dollars in US currency. I wonder which, he murmurs, in my dream, is mine. And is it feeling trapped in there too?

I think about that memory a lot, so much that it seems to be my own. And I want to be accountable to the contents of the cargo on the Cubana de Aviación turboprop aircraft that would arrive, an hour later, as foreign goods. The flags that looked like kites and the kites that surely still hang there, somewhere above a progression of terraces with a view of La Gran Piedra. Since all the children are gone.

If I were asked, likewise, to schematize my studio apartment's kitchen cabinets, I'd begin with the top shelf. The top shelf is a wasteland, a rolling, treeless plain uninhabited by the urges of both subjects and objects, an abyss containing bodies that can barely be glimpsed and which will not soon be touched. The top shelf is a place in my mind for things I no longer believe I need. A place, perhaps, for old images, images depleted of possession, the urges of posterity, anxious only to be inserted and enjoyed.

The top shelf makes me feel uneasy, as if, while inventing order within my kitchen cabinets, I've forgotten what it is I look like.

In the mirror I scan for evidence of the chia seeds I've just eaten. I smile wide, my cheeks aspiring to the lower lids of my eyes. The chia seeds have infiltrated my teeth. No—I allow the chia seeds safe passage and refuge; I allow the chia seeds to sublet my gums without reimbursement. So that when I smile, ebony pearls should leak out from my emptied gaze. Since the important thing—haven't you heard?—in electronic information is no longer the storage but the display.

The smell of blood, the metallic oil vapor of blood from my oft-bitten cuticles arouses me until I place my palm on my notebook and flip the paper, feeling the folded edge of each creamed page to calm down. My careful inventorying of the day's graces and violences.

haven't you, I
often ask myself

wondered why
soft meat

must be raised
in darkness?

In a prerecorded video lecture, I asked my students: What do you desire more—being seen or being known? What do you fear more? I later mentioned the curious case of being seen without being known or known without being seen, since recognition is not, not exactly knowledge, since being seen could mean an undisclosed intimacy, and when asked how, at an advanced age, he was able to keep his youthful look, the author answered simply that he knew how to give orders to his body.

I am a child once again when it's time to see my grandmother. She does not visit often. The cabinets come alive at her return. She knows the shelves better than I do, understands the vagaries of top-shelf weather patterns. I wear my holiday pajamas and mama's apron, which says, in Polish, "I'm not yelling—I'm Polish!" I grab a wooden spoon and pose for a picture with abuela, who has been dead for twenty-eight years this October. There is flour on the table and we are both smiling, palms flattened on the granite counter. Who is behind the camera? Who is taking the photo for which we remain here, setting a mood to place before the mind for consideration? The eerie feeling the cabinets bring subsides. Perhaps all these dark impressions are really moments of yearning.

And then I remember what I could never possibly remember, which was my parents' lives before I was born. And the way they met—at a bank, during work; each teller seated behind a window that made a hollow sound, like a penny falling in space, if you pressed your finger to the glass and tapped—and how they'd have had to say hello amid that din that felt like silence, how they had to use a common tongue, which sounded unfamiliar in each of their throats, and how they kept their relationship a secret, from even their closest friends, but also how they kept their own pasts a secret, even from each other, how mama turned her gray stockings inside out every other day of the work week, and how dad feigned ignorance if a cruel customer asked him to speak Spanish, if they asked him to speak English, and how hard it must have been for them to begin a new life when the old lives were still continuing, elsewhere, across oceans that were no longer mappable; the impossibility of restoring an origin, which was my own fear, my own desire.

So I am the only thing I could have been, born of two people who had to live by disappearing themselves, little by little, as each day passed in this new world that was created to forget the old; I, too, learned to tune a different voice for every setting, play a different bit, put on a different face. And what a monster I had to become, what a monster I am, so used to only ever existing on the outside that the inside of me so soon got sucked out … and I hardly even noticed; and the others, too: how no one ever noticed a thing.

But for that hypnotic mantra grafted, as one would come to expect, on the picture track: *He is no one because he wants to be no one and to be no one you have to be everywhere and nowhere.*

What do you desire more, I repeat, reading aloud from my own notes, being seen or being known? What do you fear more?

To be loved isn't it is to be chosen. Look at me. Look at me. Look at me, mama. Look at me, I might have said. Look at me and see me, I'll say, when I flip this photo over and write someone else's name on its bare back. Look at me and see me. And love me anyway.

sans soleil

And how I wondered what words could do, or even how silence was at a time the only way I could have spoken. And how, then, I spoke, repeating the same words I so often announced as a child: *my eyes are tired, my head is loose*—when would I really need no one else in the room to believe it? I fear you like I fear myself, the certain uncertainty of opening up, as any other body in which I've slid above or below, the hide I've prepared for use (to save myself from flight, or the impossibility of evasion). To want even to be present at my own defacement, to collapse into what I could never be if it were only me looking. Something I have never had a name for.

berlin alexanderplatz (2020)

The first night I am Laurence Olivier. For the remaining eight, which includes today, I am sleeping inside Stewart Granger. And even as I am within him, his photo—a black and white glamour portrait—sits above me, affixed to the mantel above my bed. I sleepwalk too: an evening in which I waltz into the door that belongs to my neighbor—Peter Sellers—surprised to find a dim, cool darkness that isn't mine and a keycard that opens every door or every door I've tried at the Hollywood Media Hotel, where the ghosts of film penetrate material reality, populating the room names, the interior of rooms, the hallways of floors, the floors themselves. The fitness center and spa is called Cleopatra, whose entrance is heralded by a museal plaque describing her life in German. Adjacent, a set of suites: *Lawrence Von Arabien* and *Frühstück bei Tiffany*. Inside Kurfürstendamm 202, Hollywood and history are conflated, incidentally attesting that they have only ever been the same.

After the movie, everyone suddenly becomes aware of their own body again and, as if to testify to the repossession, convulses in a fit of coughs, sneezes, hiccups, yawns.

applause of the skin against
itself

a performance
piece about my mouth

in berlin
called *wand-herr-lust*

(unprotected sex
as the last

true risk among
the bourgeoisie)

Imagined memory:
At about 7 AM their time I hid my cloud-burdened erection under the blanket and suffocated the côte de boeuf before it could be eyed or ordered.

Someone said PhD students make the best spies; someone said the only solution to the growing popularity of revenge porn is copy-righting your own body parts; someone said you can't read my work without first picturing what it is I look like, and I said look—

Isn't it the same for anyone? When the writing's good I wanna do something more than only read the words.

to be other than also and extra
to be always
everything

Sometimes it is necessary to forget (one's self) in order to tell one's story.

To allow myself to be subdued, conquered, only so that I can pay tribute to the internal rhythms and industrial design of your body, the panting glyph of emoji.

(if I knew what this writing was about I wouldn't
write it)

I heard translation is the quickest way to get out of the confines of one's self. And I wanted them to know what I could become so far from home, a succession of discontinuous positions nevertheless connected through coordinates I would have to draft, shaky handheld camera moving through these crowds as if the wind—nothing else gives you the sensation of being there more clearly—the texture of your palm over my spine on a single spring night, how every excess pretends a lack and every lack pretends an excess.

It is this desire to be drawn and drawn in, to be sidetracked, distracted, deviated, to be detoured, to be delivered with(in) indefinite coordinates; it is this desire to be touring, and also: to be the tour. Unnameable drift, or only the smell of distant bodies in movement. Writing the city means to also be written by the city, elevated and at the same time suspended in a ragged discontinuity I can't help but bow to, eyes shut so I might keep this pose a while longer, eyes open so I might see you looking.

(passing notes is like online dating but in real life)

Remember: pups think in terms of tenderness, adults in terms of passion.

My only gift: to have the confidence in believing the fallacy of every word I ever write. Which is to say their openness to critique and rupture by the reader-listener. Every word has confidence, taking into account the secret correspondence we each have with words.

(I love imagining the layers under a painting, the drafts behind a poem)

Original sin as the original glitch. Being led astray assumes a disruption of vision that completely changes the world and our recognition of its processes.

It's not only cars and markets that crash. Sometimes bodies. Sometimes the histories they carry.

Even before I typed the first words and saw how they appeared on screen I was disguised by them, finding myself, instead, to be at the whim of each letter, divorced and foreign, and how they sounded in a long straight line.

It will be a while before I learn to break them, I always think, and turn the screen into something like a canvas.

code/a

certified copy

As I write or because I write, I listen. The soundtrack is today

the twitch of my body as it warms itself, a fruitless exercise but not without reward. I listen; I am still listening. There is pain and there is difficulty. There is the notion of receding, of being recent, of the knowledge of my body's difficulty in distinguishing the moment of convergence. Of what is receding and what is recently understood as being already gone. And isn't what I've always been after—before

this began—a mode of composition that advances through coincidence? One becomes two; two becomes one. The difference is or has become the inability for me to tell the two apart; every composition as the organization of tempo; to know the moment of cleaving, the rate of motion or activity before I am to be received. I want to see things as they are, to saw language from etymology, its history of ownership. Ideas about fidelity, filiation, nationality, origin, et cetera. Prism is a medium that distorts, slants, or colors whatever is viewed through it, a word ferried from the Greeks, meaning *to saw*. Eyes like a butter knife, how the edges suddenly soften, how the blurry body starts to foam.

I want to disclaim, while insisting upon generosity. No notion of the singular without an awareness of profusion. In an earlier book, I failed at cutting my face out of every photograph in which my face appeared, or disappeared. It reminded me that a picture is worth a thousand words; it's worth a void.

One thing I've never been told is that my desires are moderate. I remember my childhood; the things I saw and read, of an attraction to strangers, discrepancy, trespass; *Quantum Leap*. The idea of experiencing life in another body, then back to yours, the brief interlude of familiarity, or estrangement; a hiccup in time or temptation; to temporarily take the place of other people to correct historical mistakes.

Something in your demeanor, I remember thinking, made me a likely suspect. Something in your demeanor, I write down, made me unlikely to acquiesce. When asked to compose a list of things I know to be true, things I know to be not true, I could only come up with falsehoods. My papers, on the other hand, are in order. I know a heart, too, is a flawed organ. I know that a good breakfast is important. I know a good German lunch is on the mind of an anonymous inquirer, who posed the question on the twenty-second of June, in 2017, a retroactive question, an answer from the future, which landed on my screen as I write or because I write, when to be current is to be *of late*. I know a German father, according to a German daughter, has always liked having warm meals for lunch and cold meals for breakfast and dinner. When we went there a few years ago, the typical day looked like this:

I stop reading because the pressure is too great; I stop because I have to, because the tension of dislocation entangles, because the face of the earth and the earth is a face, and nerves in the face interact, act upon each other, disperse. Because fragmentation continues to cut until it fashions a focal point, a sharpening of our attention even as the rest retreats, or is abandoned. Jaw of familial belonging, to be of and never in the two countries from which I emerged. The first, the first, the first to be born here, and another second

passes, indescribably (I've paused to rest). Information's drift toward entropy. Attracted to my message's affinity for deleting meaning as it passes on. (The crush of image and sound mingling.) Am I still a visual person, even as my eyes advance toward deterioration? When I get off, it is always visual, it is always with the intent—the requirement—to see the body in its rhythmic milking, the unfastening of clarity, to no longer know—to not want to know—where one body ends. When one body ends. I know that when I sleep, I don't leave so much as I arrive. I know I was a courtesan, from the ages of twenty-one through thirty-six, which is three months from now. A string of unnamed days, if I am alive outside this text, where I still live. I know I always stay till the very end.

acknowledgments

Thank you, S and J, Zosia and Juan, Sophie and John: Mom and Dad. How many versions of a life one can lead, and the many different stories that mark our passages in time and space; the discrepancies, too, that get passed down in transmission, when even static has a name, when even noise carries uncounted data. I hope you like what I did with our home movies.

Thank you to Lilly, for your mindfulness and your sensitivity; you are the best listener I know. Thank you to the team at CLASH Books, and especially Leza Cantoral and Christoph Paul, for all your tenacity and exuberance and imagination, for your unparalleled affinity for nurturing the non-normative and celebrating the experiments that harvest under the scope of a wide (a very wide) lens. Thanks, too, to Kaitlyn Kessinger and Angela Capovani for your keen eyes and editorial wisdom. Thank you to Matthew Revert for re-recording *VHS* as a graphic design that celebrates the text's desires for displacement and discrepancy. Many of these chapters were originally written in response to the prompts I also assign to my students. I am grateful for each of you, who have sustained my practice and my pleasure in the written word throughout the last several years. I'm indebted to my instructors and mentors and the many writers with whom I've kindled companionship, so many of whom have also served as initial readers for the videocassettes that constitute this novel. Meena Alexander, Wayne Koestenbaum, Mary Ann Caws, Giancarlo Lombardi, Steven Kruger, Erik Rasmussen, Miciah Hussey, Michael Kazepis, Guy Bennett, Atsuro Riley, Patrick Davis, Clif Hayward, Jay Gao, Guy Aroch, Rockwell

Harwood, Ricardo Wilson, Stu Watson, Davon Loeb, J. Mae Barizo, Caroline Hagood, Kelley Kreitz, Ryan Tracy, Harol Baez, who photographed my plunging portrait for "A Bigger Splash." I am forgetting too many people whose guidance made this story possible, whose encouragement made this book a reality. Thank you, also, to the editors and readers of the following journals, edited volumes, and anthologies, where the sequences collected in this book, sometimes in different versions, first appeared:

"bloodsport," *The Adroit Journal* 46 (2023)
"dead poets society," *Chróma* 1 (2017)
"the big ship (musical interlude)" and "l'avventura," *Corium* 20 (2015)
"good time," *Denver Quarterly* 58.2 (2024)
"l'avventura," *Duende* 3 (2015)
"my fair lady (1993)," *fluland* (July 27, 2017)
"a history of violence," *Palimpsest* 8 (2017)
"[a trailer]," "dead poets society," "from russia with love," and "blow-up," *Paris Lit Up* 12 (2024)
"roman holiday," *Pithead Chapel* 5.3 (2016)
"field of dreams," "bloodsport," and "blow-up," *Revel* 1 (Winter 2024)
"field of dreams" and "man without a face," *Revel* 2 (Summer 2024)
"eastern promises," *RHINO* 45 (2021)
"pájaros de verano," *RHINO* 46 (2022)
"let the right one in," *Social Text* (May 18, 2022)
"vision quest," *Spectacle* (2023)

Perhaps it is never too late to give breath back to the stories that have made us who we are, and in reentering our own source code, we might recast the whole.

About the Author

Chris Campanioni was born in Manhattan and grew up in a very nineties New Jersey. He is a recipient of the Pushcart Prize, the International Latino Book Award, and the Academy of American Poets College Prize. His essays, poetry, and fiction have been translated into Spanish and Portuguese and have found a home in several venues, including *Latin American Literature Today* and *Best American Essays*. His work on regimes of surveillance, queer migration, and the auto-archival practices of people moving across transnational spaces has been awarded the Calder Prize for interdisciplinary work and a Mellon Foundation fellowship. Chris's multimedia art has been exhibited at the New York Academy of Art and the film adaptation of his poem "This body's long & I'm still loading" was in the official selection at the Canadian International Film Festival. He teaches creative writing and media studies at Pace University in New York City.

ALSO BY CLASH BOOKS

VAGUE PREDICTIONS & PROPHECIES
Daisuke Shen

THE KING OF VIDEO POKER
Paolo Iacovelli

THE MAN WHO SAW SECONDS
Alexander Boldizar

THE RACHEL CONDITION
Nicholas Rombes

GENDER/FUCKING
Florence Ashley

THE LOGOS
Mark de Silva

ILL BEHAVIOR
M. Steven S.

BURN FORTUNE
Brandi Homan

ARSENAL/SIN DOCUMENTOS
Francesco Levato

SILVERFISH
Rone Shavers

COMAVILLE
Kevin Bigley

www.ingramcontent.com/pod-product-compliance
Lightning Source LLC
Jackson TN
JSHW081858010225
78215JS00001B/1

* 9 7 8 1 9 6 0 9 8 8 3 8 6 *